AF415187

Dreams Last

THE POTTER'S HOUSE BOOKS TWO – BOOK 23

CHLOE S. FLANAGAN

Copyright © 2021 Chloe S. Flanagan

Author Photo by Simon Hurst Photography

Scripture quotations are from New Revised Standard Version Bible, copyright © 1989 National Council of the Churches of Christ in the United States of America. Used by permission. All rights reserved worldwide.

All rights reserved. No part of this book may be reproduced or used in any manner without the express written permission of the publisher except for the use of brief quotations in a book review.

This is a work of fiction. Names, characters, businesses, places, events, and incidents are either the products of the author's imagination or used in a fictitious manner. Any resemblance to actual persons, living or dead, or actual events is purely coincidental.
ISBN: 9798721973017

NOTE FROM THE AUTHOR

The 23 books that form The Potter's House Books Series Two are linked by the theme of hope, redemption, and second chances. They are all stand-alone books and can be read in any order. Books will become progressively available from January 7, 2020.

Book 17: *Love's Healing Touch*, by Juliette Duncan

Book 18: *This Steadfast Heart*, by Kristen M. Fraser

Book 19: *Hope's Promise*, by Mary Manners

Book 20: *Season of Hope*, by Brenda S. Anderson

Book 21: *Everything Behind Us*, by Jen Rodewald

Book 22: *Her Covert Cowboy*, by Dora Hiers

Book 23: *Dreams Last*, by Chloe Flanagan

I came that they may have life, and have it abundantly.

John 10:10 (NRSV)

DREAMS LAST

1

Say something!

Jessica's brain screamed at her so loudly, it was a wonder the band couldn't hear it. Of all the ridiculous questions to stumble over at an audition!

"W-what?" She asked, trying to buy enough time for her neurons to reboot.

Dorian, lead guitarist and front man of the Solstice Riddles folk band, dipped his bushy blond eyebrows at her and repeated, "Why do you make music?"

Jessica swallowed. How could a simple question be so complicated? Everything had been going well. As soon as she'd stepped onto the stage of the tiny Manhattan theater where the audition was being held, she'd sensed the potential for a good rapport with the band. They'd asked about her influences and had compared notes with her on favorite songs by the artists and groups they mutually admired. When prompted, she'd talked about how her style and tastes aligned with the band's while being eclectic enough to help them expand their repertoire. Her responses and follow-up questions had been met with smiles and nods.

But through all of it, Dorian had remained silent until he leaned forward, cutting Tyrell, the drummer off mid-sentence to ask, "Why do you make music?"

Jessica stared down at her guitar and absently tapped on the tuning pegs without adjusting them. No need for that. She'd tuned the instrument before coming on stage.

She rattled off a quick, silent prayer for help. Raising her head again, she found all eyes firmly fixed on her. Heat spread over her face.

"I never knew my dad," she blurted out a little too loudly. Clearing her throat, she continued in a more moderate tone. "I mean he died before I was born. But my mom always told me music was his passion, and that he'd passed it on to me. When I was six, she gave me a guitar and some lessons for Christmas. I guess I really took to it."

Her throat expanded, and words came out smoother as the memories returned. "My mom was so proud that I loved to play and sing. She always said she couldn't wait to watch me become a professional some day. But then she died too, over two years ago, just before my seventeenth birthday. So I decided—" She paused and stood up straighter. "I decided it was time to follow the dream."

Although the faces looking back at her were sympathetic, it was a relief when Dorian changed the subject by asking her to start off with a solo. He gave her a choice from the folk standards in the band's setlist, which they'd emailed her before the audition.

As she played the opening chords of "Barbara Allen," quiet settled over her mind. Talking about her parents had stirred a throbbing ache in her heart, and she poured it into the tragic ballad's lyrics, closing her eyes at the most poignant parts: "Sweet William died of love for me, and I will die of sorrow."

The room was silent when the song ended. The expressions around her ranged from serene to solemn. Mila, one of the band's two fiddle players brushed at her eyes. Dorian gave a firm nod. "Okay. Let's do some together."

After a brief warm-up, they played two Solstice Riddles originals that were slow, melancholy tunes, one with Dorian singing the lead, and the other with Jessica. By the middle of the first song, Jessica was really starting to connect with the other musicians. It would take practice and time for them to be completely cohesive, but this was a promising start.

The rest of the band must have thought so too, because they were smiling and chatting after the second song ended.

Dorian clapped his hands once. "Okay, guys. How about a change of pace?" The corners of his bearded mouth twitched. The others began to snicker.

"The sunshine song?" Tyrell asked.

Jessica nodded, mostly to herself. They were talking about another one of the band's originals, a simple yet bright, happy love song they liked to close their gigs with, judging from the videos she'd watched.

Dorian faced her. "You take this one again."

She began playing the song. Like the other ones, she had learned and practiced it in preparation for the audition. But her voice didn't soar like she knew it could, or even like the band's former singer, whom she'd been watching on the video. The cheerful, silly lyrics seemed to take up all her breath and then some.

Still, she played each chord and sang each note exactly as she'd practiced. Not her best, but at least good enough to show them she could do it.

When the song was over, the room was quiet again. The other musicians exchanged awkward glances. Yes, she was good enough, so why did it feel like she'd sucked all the energy out of the room with a straw?

Dorian spoke up. "Okay, cool. You know? I think we've done enough today. Jessica, thanks for coming in. It's been a pleasure."

Wow. Was it that bad?

Had she really derailed the audition and blown her chance with one song?

Her stomach sank and swished as Dorian escorted her out of the rehearsal hall and down the corridor toward the exit. Abruptly, she stopped and turned toward him. "Dorian, look, I know I didn't get that last song right, but I can do better. I know I can. I just need more practice and—"

"It's not about practice, Jessica. There was nothing technically wrong with your playing or singing. And, as for the other songs, you were remarkable. The way you breathed out all that pain and sadness was authentic. More real than anyone else we've heard so far. But we're not just about that. We believe our music should speak to all of life. You know what I'm saying? The low and the high. The serious and the absurd. It's what people need. You can't spend your whole life standing up there singing to your ghosts."

Jessica winced. That was harsh. An immediate argument jumped to the tip of her tongue, but she pulled it back at the last second. The truthfulness of his words poured over her like cold rain.

"Yeah . . ." Her voice cracked, so she tried again. "Yeah, I think I see what you mean. Thank you for giving me a chance."

He sent her a kind smile that she barely managed to mirror before turning to push the door open and hurry outside before he could see the moisture form in the corner of her eyes.

2

The subway doors screeched shut right before the train lurched forward. Jessica plopped onto a seat and stared out the window for a moment before pulling out her phone. She opened the text conversation she'd had earlier in the day with her boss, Clifton, and reread it.

Jessica: I loaded the drawings and estimates for the Anderson project on a flash drive, and I'll get it to you later this afternoon. We can open the files then too, in case you have questions.

Clifton: Thanks. And I already have a question.

Jessica: What is it?

Clifton: Why are you texting half an hour before your audition? You need to be getting ready!

Jessica sat back and smiled. Most bosses wouldn't be so encouraging of an employee chasing after a music career on the side. But Clifton was more than a boss, really. After working with him for just a year, the kind, middle-aged architect and his wife Darla were like family.

She returned her attention to the texts.

Jessica: I'm on my way out now. I just wanted to be sure to tell you about the flash drive.

Clifton: Okay. Why don't you bring it to the apartment around 5 o' clock? Natalie and Glen are coming over for dinner and you can join us. It'll be a nice way to celebrate a spectacular audition.

Jessica: What if it's not spectacular?

Clifton: Then dinner can be culinary therapy. Don't sweat it. Just come on over. If you get here before we do, you can use your spare key.

Jessica: Thanks, boss.

Clifton: Of course. Now go knock 'em slightly unconscious.

Jessica: ???

Clifton: Well, you won't be able to play with them if you knock 'em dead.

Jessica: Yeah, I doubt they'd be *grateful* for that.

Clifton: . . .

Clifton: Ha! Grateful! That's a good one. Now, please get going. You're gonna do great.

You're gonna do great.
The words haunted Jessica as she exited the subway station and walked the few blocks to Clifton and Darla's apartment building. She stopped at a corner grocery on the way and bought a liter of the specialty Italian soda she'd seen them drink before. The least she could do to repay all that misplaced confidence was not show

up for dinner empty-handed.

No one was at the apartment when she arrived, so she used her spare key. Once she'd placed the flash drive on Clifton's desk and the soda on the kitchen counter, she sat down to wait. But sitting in the quiet only brought back thoughts of the failed audition, so she stood up to explore her surroundings. She walked around the large, urban loft-style living space that doubled as Darla and Clifton's home offices.

Darla's side was neat and orderly, with every folder and pen in place, but Clifton's desk was a little more haphazard and littered with dozens of drawings in progress. On a shelf above his desk sat a model of a two-story brick house. It was a replica of the first project Clifton had ever designed. Darla had gotten the model made from old drawings as a Christmas present for Clifton.

The model looked like the perfect traditional home. Jessica traced the air in front of the house with her finger: downstairs living room windows, behind which, she could almost picture a small family sitting around a coffee table laughing and playing a board game. Would life have been like that if her dad had lived? Would her mom have stayed sober and stable?

Her breath shuddered unexpectedly, and she backed away to sit back down. Reaching into her shoulder bag, she pulled out the only photo she had of her father and pondered it.

She would never get to experience that special connection with him and her mom together as a family. They were both gone. And she'd actually thought she could cling to them with her music.

What a joke! Dorian had been right. She'd been spending her life playing for ghosts.

The swish of the opening front door startled Jessica to her feet, causing her to drop the photo.

Darla walked in and raised a brow at her jumpiness. "Hey, Jessica."

"Oh, hi. Clifton told me to come inside if you all weren't here yet. I hope you don't mind."

Darla chuckled. "Of course not. Besides, he told me you'd be here so I wouldn't be alarmed, but apparently, I wasn't the one he needed to worry about."

"Yeah, I guess I was lost in thought."

Darla spotted Jessica's flyaway photo then, and gingerly bent down to pick it up.

Jessica hurried over. "I'm sorry about that."

Darla glanced at the photo as she handed it over. "Friend of yours?"

"My dad."

"Really?" Darla looked from the image to Jessica and back to the image again, her eyebrows furrowed.

Jessica shrugged. "Yeah, I favor my mom in just about every way . . . except for the music thing."

All at once, her eyes begin to burn. She blinked hard, but it didn't stop the tears from forming.

Darla stepped closer. "What's wrong, dear?"

The gentle affection in the older woman's voice was too much. With a noisy sob, Jessica crumpled onto the sofa, a messy bundle of grief and embarrassment. She hated crying in front of other people, but she couldn't seem to help herself. Shoot, it wasn't even the first time Darla had seen her hysterical.

Just as Darla sat down beside her, the front door swung open again, and Natalie walked in. "I was trying to knock, Darla, but the door was open so—"

Natalie paused, her pretty face crinkling in a frown when she saw Jessica. "Jessica, are you okay?" She placed a few grocery bags on the floor and hurried to the sofa.

Jessica looked up in time to see Natalie make a face at Darla and mouth, "What did you do?"

Darla responded with an indignant glare.

Jessica giggled in spite of herself. "She didn't do anything, Natalie. Nobody did. It was the audition." She swiped at her eyes and forced her voice not to get watery again.

Darla produced a box of tissues and offered it to her while Natalie sat down on her other side. When Jessica was more composed, she briefly recounted the audition. Once she'd finished, she rubbed her forehead.

"I feel bad, Natalie, I know you pulled some strings to get me that chance, and then I completely blew it." Jessica awkwardly folded and unfolded the tissue on her lap as she recalled her shock and excitement when Natalie had helped her get an audition with the Solstice Riddles. They were one of the most well-known, up and coming folk groups in New York. Even though Natalie was a stage actress—an increasingly famous one—she had numerous connections in the local music world too. Thanks to her close friendship with Darla, she'd been glad to pass Jessica information on gigs and auditions when she heard about them, but this had been the biggest opportunity so far. It was *too big* for Jessica, obviously.

Natalie broke into Jessica's fretting by saying, "Hey, Jessica. Look at me." When Jessica did, Natalie smiled. "You don't need to feel bad. And you can't look at the gigs you don't get as failures. Every audition is a chance to get better, learn to be a better performer, and learn something about yourself as an artist."

"I think I definitely did the last part," Jessica mumbled. Dorian's words returned to her thoughts. *You can't keep singing for ghosts.*

Natalie patted her hand and stood up to take the groceries to the kitchen. Jessica stood too and reached for a bag to help.

"Then use what you learned for the next time," Natalie continued. "And there will be a next time. Do you know how many parts I've gotten compared to how many I've tried out for?"

Jessica shrugged and placed a bag on the kitchen counter.

Natalie began pulling fresh vegetables from the bags. "Let me put it this way: if my career were a salad, the parts I wasn't right for would be the lettuce and the roles I landed would be the tomatoes." She leaned forward and winked. "And a few of *those* were rotten."

Jessica's snicker turned into an outright chuckle when Darla joined them in the kitchen and said, "Are we talking about performing or dinner now?"

The front door swung open once again as Clifton entered, followed by Natalie's fiancé, Glenn. A bustle of activity ensued as everyone pitched into help with dinner preparations under Natalie's direction. In addition to being a talented actress, she had top-notch kitchen skills.

Darla or Natalie must have texted the men about Jessica's botched audition, because neither Glenn nor Clifton mentioned it. However, Clifton did approach Jessica during a lull in the preparations to offer a hug, which she gratefully accepted. Something about the embrace and being surrounded by the laughter and banter of the group of friends put her world to rights again. Was this what it was like to be part of a family? A family that actually acted like family, that is. An image of her aunt Lois came to mind, with her tall, elegant frame, perfectly styled, shoulder length blonde hair, and disapproving eyes. Jessica gave her head a slight shake. Now was not the time to think about *her* on top of everything else.

3

Thunder crackled through the air, and rain gushed from the sky like someone had turned on the celestial faucet full blast. The lights above Lois's desk flickered for the third time that afternoon and finally went off entirely, cloaking the room in partial darkness. She raised her head from her blank computer screen and shivered.

After a fruitless moment of waiting and hoping the electricity would kick back on, she stood and went to the window to open the blinds wider. It didn't provide much light, though, thanks to another summertime Texas storm.

Making her way to her office door, she opened it. Overlapping voices greeted her; some screeched, some complained, and some giggled nervously in the darkness. Lois stepped into the hall and assumed her serene yet firm, authoritative tone. "Okay, everyone, stay calm please!"

The other voices drifting through the town hall office hushed, causing Lois to smirk just a bit. It's almost as if they were waiting for her, as city manager, to be the voice of reason.

"Stay where you are until the emergency generator comes on," she continued. "We don't want anyone to trip and fall in the dark."

A moment later, light flooded the building, and the offices began to buzz with activity. Lois took a deep, fortifying breath. Her already heavy workload had likely just increased, if the power outage was widespread across town.

As she suspected it would, her office phone began to ring. She turned away from the doorway and headed toward her desk.

"Ms. Connell!" A voice boomed behind her. She winced. Barry Morton. Of course the most demanding city council member would pick this moment of total chaos to show up in her office. She painted on a welcoming smile and swiveled to face him.

"Mr. Morton. How nice to see you. What brings you out on such a miserable day?" she asked, tilting her head toward the window, where sheets of rain still buffeted the pane.

"Hmph. Same thing that always brings me out these days: the zoning vote. I heard Roberts *still* isn't on board!"

Her smile widened. "I don't know who your source is, but that's actually inaccurate. After he and I talked for some time yesterday, Mr. Roberts decided to cooperate after all."

Morton's bushy gray eyebrows dipped then shot up. "He did?"

"Oh, yes. He sees the logic behind it and is ready to move forward."

"Hey. That's great! I mean, wow!" Morton shook his head. "I can't believe it. How did you make him see reason?"

Lois flapped her hand dismissively. "I didn't do anything but talk it through with him. However, Mr. Roberts has one small stipulation. He asked that we move on the new city park proposition next month."

She threw in the last part like an afterthought when, in reality, she'd all but promised Roberts to help him make it happen.

Morton scowled. "Roberts, you cheeky jerk," he muttered under his breath before returning his focus to Lois. "That's all he wants?"

Taking a seat on the edge of her desk, Lois crossed her arms and sent Morton a conspiratorial grin. "That's all. I think he knows you have the stronger position here, not to mention the best interest of the town at heart. No one can argue with that."

Morton flashed a smug smile. "I guess he does at that. And you helped him see it, didn't you?"

Lois gave the appropriate self-deprecating shrug.

"No, you did. I'm sure of it." Morton stuck out his hand to shake hers. "I had my doubts about a woman your age taking this position, Ms. Connell. What are you, barely forty? But I can see what an asset you are."

She thanked him and exchanged the necessary pleasantries, her mind still half occupied with everything she needed to do, until Morton finally indicated he was ready to leave. On his way out, he sent her one more nod, an unmistakable look of respect flashing through his eyes.

Respect.

She gave her head an incredulous shake as she returned to her desk. But instead of sitting, she paused to examine the photographs lining her credenza. The first few were photos she'd taken of town landmarks. They were good shots. Nice lighting and contrast. She liked to think she captured not only buildings, but the life and history within them too. It had been so long since she'd done anything like that.

The rest of the photos were of people: pictures of her and the mayor with the governor and various senators.

Yes, there could be no question she was respected now. Her. Lois Connell, oldest daughter of the town drunk. It had taken most of her forty years, but she'd finally made people forget about that. She finally had admiration and esteem instead of pity and ridicule.

Her gaze fell on one more photo, as if her subconscious were determined to contradict her. It was the only picture in her office of her niece Jessica. It had been taken at a city holiday party a few years before, when Jessica was fifteen. She was sitting by herself, away from the rest of the partygoers, shoulders slumped, arms folded, as if she wanted to curl up and disappear or escape. Jessica had never appreciated Lois's position in the town. Never realized how lucky she was to grow up with the advantages Lois had given her after Lois's sister had all but abandoned the girl. Instead, Jessica seemed to resent her.

The shrill ring of her office phone brought a welcome respite from her thoughts. Lois scrambled to answer, not even caring if it was some citizen calling to announce their electricity was out, as if she were directly responsible for all the utilities in town. It happened every time there was a power outage, but no matter. She'd answer questions and provide competent directions as always. Like most things in life that didn't involve her niece: this was a situation she had completely under control.

"Lois Connell, City Manager," she answered.

"Yeah, this is Gary."

She blinked. Gary? He may be her nearest neighbor, but they rarely spoke. "Yes, Gary. What can I do for you?"

"The creek level is rising. I'm pretty sure your place is gonna flood."

4

"Why don't you sit down and stay a minute, Jessica? You don't have to help with the dishes then run off like a charwoman."

Jessica smirked before turning to Darla and affecting an exaggerated cockney accent. "I appreciate it, missus, but I've got washin' and ironin' of me own back 'ome."

Clifton guffawed and Darla grinned and patted the sofa beside her. The couple had moved to the living room once the dishes were all done and Natalie and Glenn had left.

Jessica sat. "I'll stay for a minute, but it must be getting late." She pulled out her phone to confirm the time and frowned at the sight of multiple notifications on the screen.

"Something wrong?" Darla asked.

Jessica studied the screen. "Oh, I still get notifications from the local news stations back in Texas. It looks like they've had some pretty intense storms today. Hail, flooding, even a tornado or two."

Clifton and Darla scooted to the edge of their seats. Clifton asked, "Is everything okay?"

The muscles in her forehead tensed and throbbed under her frown. "It's hard to say. The story says there's a lot of damage and a few injuries." She looked up. "I guess I should call my aunt."

But calls to both Lois's cellphone and house went unanswered.

Darla reached over and squeezed her hand. "Don't worry."

Don't worry. Don't worry.

Her brain chewed the words the way her teeth chewed her bottom lip. Was she worried? Did she think Lois could be hurt?

No, she didn't think that. Her insides wouldn't feel so numb if she really suspected that, would they?

Clifton was talking now. "She probably lost electricity if the storms were that bad. Her cell battery could be dead. Is there someone else you can call?"

"Marty and Barb," she blurted out, and her stomach turned over as she pictured the two sixty-something women. That old roadhouse they ran would crumble under a good, strong wind, let alone a tornado. At least they had a basement. If they'd been working when the storm hit, had they managed to get in it?

Jessica snatched up her phone, fingers shaking as she scrolled for the number. One ring. Two. Three. Four. *Lord, please.*

"Hey, Jess," Marty's low, sandpaper voice greeted her matter-of-factly. "Tired of the Big Apple yet?"

Jessica squeezed her eyes shut and grinned in relief. "Never mind that, Marty. How are you?"

"Me?"

"Yeah, the storms. They've been on the news. How's the town? Have you heard anything about Lois, by any chance?"

"Oh, well, it was pretty hairy for a little while, but everything here is okay. Barb went out to find out how everyone else is and— oh, here she is." Her voice sounded far away like she'd put down the phone. "Barb, honey, it's Jess. She heard about the storms and wants to know if we know anything about her aunt."

The phone rustled. "Jess, sweetie, hello."

If Marty's voice was sandpaper, Barb's was soft like a wool sweater. "I've been walking around town. Most of the buildings are fine except for some damage here and there, but your aunt's place flooded."

"Flooded? Well, is Lois . . . "

"She's fine, Jess. She was at work when it happened, but I'm sorry to say it's a big mess. I imagine it'll take some time to sort it all out."

Once Jessica was off the phone, she repeated what Barb had told her.

Clifton and Darla discussed the news, and asked questions, which she tried to answer. But all the while, thoughts of Lois, all alone with her damaged house, swarmed through Jessica's mind. They prodded and poked at her brain, like the sound of her morning alarm when she wasn't ready to wake yet.

"Clifton, do you think I can have some time off? I mean, I don't need to be completely off. I'll take my laptop and can probably do most of the stuff I do now. It's just . . . I think I should probably go see if my aunt needs help."

Clifton sent her an understanding smile. "Of course. I would've suggested it myself if you hadn't."

Darla's forehead crinkled. "When's the last time you talked to your aunt?"

"I call her every month or so." Always in the middle of a weekday afternoon, when Jessica was almost certain Lois would be unavailable to talk, but she left that part out.

"Every month," Darla mused, before standing up. "I just realized I need to take care of something right quick." She stood and squeezed Jessica's shoulder. "You're a good egg."

Jessica waved off the odd but unmerited compliment as Darla quit the room.

She continued to chat with Clifton for a few more minutes then stood to leave. She had to get ready for her trip after all. That would mean packing and getting online to buy a bus ticket. It would take hours and hours to get to Texas that way, but she couldn't afford a plane ticket on such late notice.

As she left, she accepted her second hug of the evening from Clifton and one from Darla.

"Call us when you get there, please," Clifton said.

Once she was back at the small apartment she shared with two roommates, Jessica sat down at her computer to search for bus tickets. But before she did, she checked her email and saw there was an email from Darla.

Why would she email when Jessica had just seen her?

Her eyes widened as she scanned the message, which simply read: **Don't worry about it.**

Attached to the email was an electronic ticket for a flight to Midland, Texas scheduled for the next morning.

Jessica swallowed a gasp. Darla had bought her a ticket? Now her trip would only take a few hours, and she'd only be out the price of a car ride from Midland to the small town where her aunt lived. Immediately, she began to type out a response. But what could she say?

She couldn't refuse it. It had already been purchased. Saying, "you shouldn't have" could sound rude and ungrateful. At the very least, she would promise to pay Darla back.

But scrolling up to hit the "reply" button brought her to the first part of Darla's message. "Don't worry about it."

The kind, if sometimes meddlesome, woman had already anticipated her response.

With a sigh, Jessica typed. "I don't know what to say." That much was evident. ". . . except thank you so much. I'll never forget this."

She sent the email, and several minutes later, the reply came: "You're welcome. Safe travels."

Jessica leaned her elbow on her desk and rested her head on her hand.

Darla and Clifton had been incredibly generous to her ever since they'd first met a little over a year before. Although Jessica had been surprised, Darla's buying her a plane ticket wasn't out of character. She'd realized Jessica probably couldn't afford the ticket, yet still needed to get to Texas quickly, so she'd acted. Not only that, Darla clearly sympathized with Jessica's strained relationship with her aunt and, perhaps, even respected her decision to help anyway.

Jessica heaved a sigh and stood up to get ready for bed. Darla's respect for her decision bugged her a little.

She went to the bathroom to brush her teeth and flinched at her reflection. Darla thought she was a good person for helping her aunt, based on what Jessica had told her.

Jessica furiously began brushing her teeth as her thoughts swam.

Yes, she'd told Darla how her aunt had taken her in when her mom left, a fact for which she'd always be grateful. But she'd also explained how Lois had never let Jessica forget she was an obligation. She'd told Darla that, despite her aunt's behavior, she felt sorry for Lois.

Jessica rinsed and shuffled out of the bathroom.

What she hadn't told Darla was how, even now, she sometimes cried tears of hurt and *fury* over the whole thing. How, when she'd left her aunt's house, she'd had no real intention of ever going back. How she knew she should and would go help now, but that the thought also made her stomach sour.

Once Jessica was on her side of her bedroom, she ensured her roommate was asleep then threw herself down on her bed, tears of shame burning her eyelids.

No, she wouldn't admit so much bitterness to Darla or anyone else. But that didn't mean it was a secret. She squeezed her eyes shut and groaned. "Oh, Lord, I'm so sorry for having all these ugly feelings and thoughts. Please help me get over it and finally move on."

Quiet, like a gentle, soothing hand slowly settled over her and she began to drift off to sleep. A wry chuckle slipped out with her last bit of consciousness. She was praying to move on but, tomorrow, things would probably feel more like going backwards.

5

Lois sat hunched over the steering wheel of her Buick and studied her house. From the front, it was still the respectable, two-story structure it had always been, complete with a manicured row of hedges beneath the front window. Back when she'd first repainted the front porch and planted the greenery, she'd been so proud of her work that she'd taken several photographs to capture it. The house looked so neat and refined compared to how it had been when she was growing up. Even now, the outside was picture-perfect.

But the inside was another matter. Floodwater had flowed in from the back of her house without quite reaching the front. The serious impact was in her storage room, back bathroom, and home office. From what she could tell the night before, the beautiful hardwood floors, several boxes, and furniture legs were the chief victims of the flood.

As soon as she'd gotten news of the flooding, Lois had rushed home. Once it was safe, she'd shut off the circuit breakers for the affected rooms, and surveyed the damage. At the time, she'd been thankful the water hadn't been higher, but now, in the blistery light of day, she was overwhelmed.

The steps she needed to take to address the situation were clear and spread out before her. All that remained was for her to get up and attack them with her characteristic practicality. Yet she just kept sitting, her breath coming in heavy puffs, as if she'd been doing physical labor already. It was just so much: the burden of dealing with this mess on top of the endless stream of town business. She'd already rescheduled two meetings to be here and meet the insurance adjuster this morning.

The sound of an approaching car prevented her from falling deeper into agitation, and she looked up to see a compact car stop at the end of the street and let a passenger out of the back.

Lois squinted in the sunlight to watch the car drive away. Since when did insurance adjusters have drivers? She could just make out the form of a woman in business slacks and a white blouse walking in her direction.

Lois got out of her car and moved to greet the woman but froze as soon as she got a closer look. The young woman carried an overnight bag in one hand and a guitar case in the other. "Jessica!"

"Hi, Aunt Lois." Her niece greeted her with a bemused expression then hesitated a second before sweeping forward and planting a quick kiss to her cheek. "I'm so sorry about the flooding."

Lois took a halting step backwards. "H-how did you know?"

It was an irrelevant question but she needed a moment to process the change in Jessica. Her business casual attire made her appear older than her nineteen years, as did her confident posture. Gone were the slumped shoulders and shifting gaze of the teenage girl who had left so abruptly just a year ago. What a difference those months had made!

"What are you doing here?" Lois recovered from her surprise enough to ask when her first question went unanswered.

Jessica tucked a strand of her long, brown hair behind her ear. "I figured you might need some help with cleanup. You're always so busy."

Lois frowned. After a whole year of barely speaking, she'd decided to show up like it was the most natural thing in the world? She waved a hand at Jessica's guitar case. "I can't believe you'd abandon your pipedreams up in New York over a little water. Unless they're not panning out so well, hmm?"

Jessica's upright posture slipped, the slight curve of her mouth flattened, and for a second, she looked more like the girl Lois had always known. But then she jerked her head back and forth, as if shaking away Lois's words. "Well, I'm taking a little break from that, and I arranged to do remote work for my job with the architect. I talked about him in one of my emails, right? He has experience with doing renovations after floods and told me a few of the things you'd need help with. Like taking inventory of the stuff in the damaged rooms. It might be a good job for someone who's lived in the house."

Her voice trailed off, and she shuffled her feet.

Lois's hand clenched. *Someone who's lived in the house!* For twelve years, she'd given the girl a home, yet she made it sound like she'd been a temporary houseguest. Is that how she looked at it? "Look, Jessica. I—"

A car sporting her insurance company's logo pulled onto the street, serving to cool Lois's temper. Jessica turned to face the car and stood beside her.

Slowly, the tension in Lois's shoulders began to ease. Jessica had shown up offering to help with the very problem Lois had been bemoaning just a few minutes before. Shouting at the girl like a crotchety old aunt probably wasn't the best response.

As they walked toward the insurance adjuster's car, Lois cringed at her own petulance. Truthfully, she *had* been starting to feel older than her years lately. She racked her brain trying to remember when the feeling had begun to seep in. Had it started with a particular project at work? Something stressful that made her lose sleep, maybe?

No, her fatigue had started a year ago, when Jessica had left. How had she never made that connection until now?

DREAMS LAST

24

6

Jessica sloshed through the small room her aunt used for storage, inputting a few more items into her smartphone's note-taking application as she made her way to the back door. Two hours before, she had donned rubber boots and began photographing the rooms of the house the water had reached and taking note of significant items that were damaged. Later in the afternoon, she would organize the photos and notes on her computer.

After meeting with the insurance adjuster, Lois had gone to her office to address the most pressing of her town responsibilities for the day, but she'd assured Jessica she would be back in a few hours. That was okay with Jessica. She worked best when she was by herself.

She took another look around the storage room. She'd moved several boxes whose bases had been sitting in a layer of water. Soon, she would need to sort through their contents to see how much would need to be cleaned or thrown away. But that would be a big job and, at the moment, she needed some fresh air.

Outside, she sat down on a wrought iron bench in the front yard and picked up her guitar case, which she'd stored in the front part of the house for safekeeping. Absently, her fingers played a few chords, but no particular tune came to mind. She smirked down at her instrument, certainly nothing by the Solstice Riddles.

Her humor fizzled out as she remembered the audition. Had she truly believed an established band like that would want her in their act? It had been a ridiculous *pipedream.*

Even a couple of hours later, Lois's words still stung. She'd had zero patience or respect for Jessica's music dreams ever since the day her mom had given her that first guitar. It had been more than twelve years now, but Jessica could still picture the look of severe disapproval on Lois's face when Jessica's mom showed her the instrument and told her about her dad. Really, Lois would have that same look anytime her mom talked about Jessica's dad. It wasn't hard to figure out that her aunt had disliked the man for some reason.

Was dislike of Jessica's musician father what prompted Lois's distaste for her niece's passion for music? Whatever the cause, Lois's reaction to Jessica's goals over the years had ranged from being dismissive to outright antagonistic.

Jessica huffed a frustrated sigh and returned her guitar to its case. Lois's attitude had been one thing when Jessica had lived under her roof, but things were different now. She wasn't a burden to her aunt any more. She was here to help!

She stood and paced the front yard, her thoughts circling then narrowing. It wasn't just the music. Lois had disapproved of almost everything about Jessica for years. Who could blame her, really? Jessica had been too much for her mom to handle. The responsibility had been forced on Lois.

After a few more steps, Jessica sank back onto the bench.

Maybe she really had been a burden.

Closing her eyes, Jessica breathed in the balmy summer air and shifted under the sunbeams whose heat seemed to grow more forceful by the moment. Despite the tiny beads of sweat tickling the back of her neck, she started to doze.

Her phone buzzed then, snapping her back to attention as she glanced at the screen. *Darla.*

Jessica had texted her and Clifton after her plane landed, but she hadn't talked to them since then.

"Hi, Darla."

"Hey. How are you?"

"I'm good. I was just taking a break." She explained what she'd been doing all morning and what she still needed to accomplish.

When Jessica was finished, Darla gave a low whistle. "That must be quite a job, but it sounds like it's under control. Now, back to my original question: how are *you?*"

Jessica's insides warmed at Darla's perceptiveness. It was like she knew that the real challenges were in the things Jessica hadn't mentioned. So she talked a little about her interactions with Lois.

Darla made one or two irritated grunts while Jessica spoke, but she mostly listened without commentary.

"I don't know what I'm doing, Darla. I think the stuff I'm doing is helpful, but I really wonder if Lois would've been happier if I'd just stayed away," she finished with a sigh, hating how pathetic her tone sounded.

Darla didn't answer for a few seconds, as if she were thinking or listening to someone in the background, although Jessica didn't think anyone was there.

After a few more seconds of heavy silence, Jessica cleared her throat. "Anyway, that's how it's going. I didn't mean to whine or—"

"I want you to know something, Jessica," Darla interrupted. "You're doing the right thing. Okay? You are a bright, caring, and lovely soul. And you're doing the right thing. Don't you dare forget any of that."

Jessica's throat seized and her eyelids started to sting. "I . . ."

This time, Darla was the one to clear her throat. "I've gotta go. Call again soon, okay? Bye now."

Jessica blinked and stared at her blank phone screen. Darla was one of the most consistently kind people she'd ever met, but she sometimes reminded Jessica of a soldier in a war movie. She'd throw out a kindness grenade then jump out of the way before she could see the full impact of her actions. It was just Darla's way, and Jessica loved her for it.

When she'd left Lois's house a year ago, she couldn't have imagined meeting anyone like Darla and Clifton or the odd circumstances that had brought them all together. But for reasons she still didn't completely understand, they had chosen to make her part of their lives. And they had chosen to—

Her train of thought rolled to a stop. They had *chosen*. Darla and Clifton had made a choice to care about and include her even though she wasn't a relative. She cared about them too, of course, but her gratitude and affection seemed more like bright and inescapable feelings rather than a choice.

Jessica slumped under the weight of her thoughts. She had a lot to thank Lois for too, but she'd rarely had those warm, grateful feelings toward her aunt. Yet what did that matter? Love was a choice. Jessica could see that now. And as much as she tried to ignore it, she couldn't shake the suspicion that very few people in Lois's life had made that choice. But Jessica could . . . with some help.

Leaning forward until her elbows rested on her knees, Jessica folded her hands.

"This is new to me, Lord, but I really want to make an effort with my aunt. I think—I think she might have some hurt in her life and I don't really know how to help with that, but I do want to show her love, if I can. I want to try and show the kind of love Darla and Clifton showed me. Please help me do that."

7

Lois opened her back door and peeked inside the storage room, careful not to step in the standing water. Everything that had been on the floor was now sitting on tables and chairs covered with heavy plastic tarps for protection.

In the center of the room, Jessica stood half-turned away from the door as she rummaged through a box and swayed slightly. It was only then Lois noticed the music emanating from somewhere, probably Jessica's phone. The girl was singing along with Cass Elliot's rendition of "Dream a Little Dream," as she worked.

Jessica's voice was soft and rich, and her face thoroughly tranquil as she sang. For a moment, Lois wasn't standing outside a flooded room anymore. Instead she was upstairs checking in to ensure a six-year-old Jessica was asleep in her bed. No matter how the day had gone. How many dozens of questions Jessica had asked: demanding when her mom would come home or why they never talked about her dad. No matter how many times her childish will clashed with Lois's, the little girl always managed to look so peaceful when she slept.

As if finally sensing Lois's gaze, Jessica turned toward the door. Her face reddened and she hastily pulled her phone from her back pocket and silenced the music. Whether it was the girl's obvious discomfort about singing around her or the complete disappearance of her peaceful expression, something about Jessica's reaction to her arrival saddened Lois.

"Aunt Lois, I didn't see you there." She sent a small smile.

"How has your day gone so far?"

"Not bad. It looks like you've been productive."

Jessica's smile widened. "Well, there's still plenty of work left, but I did try to move as much stuff as possible out of the standing water without getting moisture on anything else. I also made an inventory list and took pictures."

Lois folded her arms. "And let me guess, you re-shingled the roof and cleaned out the gutters too?"

The girl's eyes widened at first then she smirked. "Nah, I was waiting until dusk for that. Thought it might be cooler."

Lois chuckled. "Well, in the meantime, why don't you get out of those rubber boots so we can grab some lunch?"

"Okay, sure."

Jessica moved away from the box she'd been looking through, revealing its contents. There was a photo album and a single VHS-C cassette with the words "Rising Sun" written on the label in neat letters. Lois drew in a sharp, almost painful breath.

"Is something wrong?" Jessica asked before following Lois's stare to the box. "Oh, yeah, the mini tape," she said with a giggle. "Did they actually make machines small enough to play these little guys?"

Lois swallowed hard. "No, i-it's a camcorder tape. There were special adaptors that allowed them to play in a VCR."

"Hmm. That's cool. Do you still have one and a VCR somewhere so you can look at this tape?"

"No, there's no need. It's not important, you can just trash it."

Jessica's mouth fell open. "Are you sure? It could be—"

"I said it's not important!" Lois snapped, prompting Jessica to take a step backward. "What I mean is, I keep all my important home videos in a plastic storage bin up in my closet. That one is probably just messed up or something. You can throw it away when we get ready to sort this stuff. Now, let's get that lunch." Lois turned and walked away without waiting to see if Jessica followed.

Once she got to her car, though, Lois did wait, taking advantage of Jessica's delay to catch a few deep breaths of fresh air. What was the matter with her? Since when did she get so upset over ancient history? What did any of it matter now?

After a few moments, Jessica joined her by the car. Lois opened her door to get inside just as a minivan and a sedan whirled past her and parked in the driveway behind her. "What in the world?"

Car doors began opening in a flurry and several people emerged, beginning with a petite, gray-headed woman that Lois immediately recognized as the new associate minister at her church. "Reverend June? What's going on?"

The older woman gave her a bespectacled grin. "Hello, Lois. How are you? We're sorry to drop in without calling, but Murphy and I heard about your flooding problem, so we recruited a few people to come over and see if you needed help with cleanup."

Lois's jaw went slack then quickly hardened. "I'm sorry for you're trouble, but it's simply not necessary. The damage wasn't that substantial, and I'm more than capable of handling it without any outside interference."

June's smile dimmed at Lois's words.

Jessica walked up beside Lois then, reminding her of the girl's presence. "*We* are more than capable, I mean," she corrected herself. "I don't think you've met my niece Jessica yet."

The two shook hands. "I'm glad to meet you, Reverend," Jessica said pleasantly. "I think the church was still searching for an associate when I left. I'm glad they filled the position. Would you excuse us?"

To Lois's surprise, Jessica swiveled to face her, placed a firm hand on her arm, and said, "Aunt Lois, can I talk to you for a second?"

Once they were a few yards away from the crowd, Jessica crossed her arms. "What's wrong?"

"Wrong?"

Jessica pursed her lips in a firm line. "That's the closest to rude I've ever heard you be with an outsider, even the most obnoxious councilmembers. And this is your minister! It's so unlike you."

Lois scowled. If the topic was uncharacteristic behavior, Jessica's confrontational attitude in that moment was a prime example. But she didn't call attention to that fact, because Jessica had a valid point.

Combing her hand through her hair, Lois turned and walked away a few steps. "I'm not trying to be rude, but I must make it clear to them that I don't need their pity! I don't need their prying, concerned eyes on me now and I never have. I never will again."

"Aunt Lois . . ."

Lois began to walk faster, speaking mostly to herself now. "I haven't given twenty years of my life to this town just to—"

"Lois, will you please relax?"

She stopped and looked at Jessica, who had placed a hand on her arm once again. Jessica's expression softened and she spoke low. "Trust me. No one pities you. You're the city manager; the town counts on you. This . . ." she gestured toward the church group. "This isn't about pity. I think it's about offering to make things easier for you because you're one of their own. But if you push them away, they'll think you're ungrateful."

Jessica leaned closer. "You didn't raise *me* to be ungrateful."

Lois stared. It was the first time she'd ever heard Jessica acknowledge the fact that she'd raised her. The cast iron vise that had closed around her heart the moment the church members had shown up slowly began to loosen. "Okay," she finally said. "I'll accept their help."

"Okay, then," Jessica replied with a satisfied half-smile.

As they returned to the group, Lois shook her head. She'd gained the upper hand with difficult personalities enough times to know she was being managed, and by a nineteen-year-old, no less. But it didn't bother her as much as she might have expected.

"Excellent!" June exclaimed when Lois agreed to the assistance. "We can help you sort through your water logged belongings, and Murphy is on his way with another helper and a sump pump so we can get rid of the standing water.

"That would be wonderful," Lois admitted.

Within minutes, the merry band of recruits was lining up outside her house, cleaning supplies and rubber boots at the ready. Despite her lingering misgivings, Lois couldn't help but smile at the bustling display of goodhearted energy.

"All we need is that sump pump now and—oh, here he is!" June said, pointing to a pickup that had just pulled in front of the house.

Lois approached the driver's side and greeted Reverend Murphy as he emerged.

"Hello, Lois!" The tall, lanky man shook her hand. "I've got just the thing we need to get rid of the water, courtesy of a new visitor who volunteered his sump pump. He's only been in town a week; can you believe that? But you know what? He said he used to live here years ago, now that I think of it."

Lois silently chuckled at the man's long-winded greeting. "I really appreciate your help, Reverend Murphy."

She sent a quick glance over her shoulder and spotted Jessica, who sent her an approving nod before hurrying to join the volunteers.

Murphy said, "It's no problem at all. This guy here is the one to thank for bringing his spare equipment to the rescue."

He pointed to the other side of the truck where the passenger door stood open.

"Lois, meet Joshua Ridgeway. Or maybe you knew him from before. He said his family lived here for years."

Her head seemed to turn by tiny increments like a stop motion movie as she looked away from Murphy and into the big blue astonished eyes of Joshua Ridgeway.

Did she know him? Once upon a time, she'd been certain she was going to marry him.

8

"You're looking well."

Countless years dedicated to proper behavior—all the manufactured smiles, polite lies, counting-to-ten deep breaths, and everything else needed to show this town she was the stable, kind, and upright polar opposite of her father—Lois required every last one of them to conjure a distant smile and voice steady enough to say those words to Joshua.

Her heart thundered in her chest. *You're looking well.* Never mind that the phrase sounded like something from a 1950s movie; at least she had gotten it out. And it was no polite lie. His blond hair had darkened to a bronze color with just the tiniest flecks of silver interspersed at the temples. He wore it clipped much shorter than he had when he was younger, giving him a serious, earnest appearance compounded by the black-rimmed eyeglasses that framed his blue eyes.

Those eyes stared at her now: wide, searching, and unreadable—they never used to be unreadable to her. He continued to stare, even as Murphy started talking again. "Well, I guess you two do know each other. That's awesome! I'll let you catch up while I unload the sump pump."

Joshua finally stepped forward. "Lois, I—" He coughed and started again. "I didn't know you would be here."

Her stomach clenched. She hadn't constructed any wild fantasies about water under a bridge, but that didn't mean she was ready for his statement or the subtext: If I'd known you would be here, I wouldn't have come.

"Murphy didn't tell you that the sump pump was for my house?" It was a good, neutral question.

He rubbed a hand over the back of his head. "No. He didn't realize I knew you. He just said one of the church members needed help with some water cleanup, so I offered the sump pump. It's from one of Dad's old warehouses. I'm selling the construction business, but there's still some stuff that needs to be sorted, now that he's gone. That's why I'm in town."

"I was sorry to hear he'd passed."

"Thanks." He shoved his hands deep into his jean pockets.

He'd done that ever since they were kids, but only when he was nervous, like the time his father caught them playing at one of his construction sites. Or that time when they were sixteen, hanging out by the creek, and he had turned to her and said . . . No! Lois clenched her fist and released it. She wouldn't let her memory wander down that path.

"I have to go back to my office now," she told him. "It was nice to see you."

"Lois, wait." He followed close behind as she walked away. She glanced over her shoulder in time to see him raise his arm as if to touch her. Her breath caught. But he stopped short and lowered his hand. "Do you think we could talk for a few minutes? If not today, maybe another time?"

What could they possibly have to talk about after all this time? Part of her wanted to ask, but the sensible, self-preserving part chose to end the conversation right away. "Yeah, sure. Another time."

****

Lois rushed past bustling desks and offices on the way to her own, barely acknowledging the other city workers, even the ones attempting to flag her down. Once inside her office, she closed the door with a dull thud and locked the door. She grabbed a bottle of water from her mini fridge and collapsed into her desk chair.

For a moment, she watched her reflection in her blank computer screen. There were bound to be dozens of emails in her inbox, not to mention the voice messages clamoring for her attention, judging by the red flashing light on her desk phone.

She took a long drink of water then turned on her computer to get to work. But when she raised her bottle again, her hand began to tremble under its weight. Without warning, her eyes went blurry. She swallowed a sob and put her head in her hands.

Joshua.

It had been twenty years since she'd seen him. Twenty years since he'd left town without a word or even a note to say where he was going or why. They'd been engaged for a year and together for practically all of their youth, and he'd left her alone.

Lois released a shuddering breath and swiped her tears away. No. She wouldn't cry anymore. She wouldn't indulge in self-pity. She couldn't give into the misery of the memory.

The most painful part of what had happened all those years ago was also the part that meant she had no real right to feel sorry for herself. The relationship had ended because of her. She had killed Joshua's love.

DREAMS LAST

9

"How did things go this morning?"

Knowing her aunt would only want the bottom line, as usual, when she'd called Jessica from her office asking for an update, Jessica relayed the relevant parts of the cleanup that had taken place when the church volunteers returned for a second day of work. After the summary, she concluded, "I don't think anyone from church will need to come back. Things are pretty well under control."

"Good," Lois answered quickly, which made Jessica grin. Even though she'd agreed to accept help, Lois obviously had no interest in prolonging the situation.

"Oh, and I went to the store and got a few cold cuts and things to feed the helpers before they left. You know, to show appreciation and everything."

"Hmm, yes. That was a good idea. Thanks. I'll reimburse you for whatever you were out for that."

"You don't have to. They were helping me too." Jessica shrugged, even though Lois couldn't see her over the phone and changed the subject to avoid an argument. "Did you get my email yet?"

"Yes! The spreadsheet looks good."

Jessica blinked. "Really? 'Cuz I can add some things or organize it even better by—"

"No, it's exactly what I need, as is."

"Oh. Okay. Then I'm gonna take a few boxes over to the

storage place you rented."

"Already? That's great. I'll see you later then."

Once the call ended, Jessica finished carrying boxes to the half-bed pickup truck she'd borrowed from Lois. But when she got behind the wheel, she didn't start the engine yet.

Something had been different about her conversation with Lois. There was an unusual note in her tone that had almost sounded like . . . approval. That was it. For the first time in her life, she had her aunt's approval, and it felt strange. She'd certainly never gotten it over any of her past actions, especially her music.

Jessica scoffed. Well, looking at the status of her so-called music career now, it wasn't hard to see why Lois would disapprove.

But what had happened between her and Lois today had nothing to do with music. It had simply been Jessica putting her organizational skills to use to accomplish some tasks efficiently. They were practical skills, sensible ones, skills that she could build on to become successful. And Lois, of all people, would have an appreciation for that.

Jessica waited for the usual wave of resentment, the one that always overwhelmed her when she compared Lois's priorities with her own. But the wave didn't come. There was nothing inherently wrong with Lois's push for practicality or even in her pushing Jessica toward it for so many years. Could anyone fault Lois for wanting to see her niece on a stable, productive path instead of one that led her to embarrassing herself at an audition that was probably the first of many failed auditions? Most likely, Lois had only wanted what was best for Jessica.

Her fingers squeezed around the steering wheel. Did Lois really want what was best for her? She'd never really considered it. She hadn't been willing to give her the benefit of the doubt. But it had probably been the case all along.

Despite the impact of the realization, Jessica giggled and raised her eyes skyward. "Is this what happens when I ask for help in loving someone?"

As she started the truck, her glance fell to the seat beside her, where she'd placed the photo album and miniature videotape she'd found earlier. With a sigh, she picked up the tape. She'd brought it with her because Mrs. Lucas, one of the church ladies, had seen her looking at it and had told her about a camera shop on Main Street that could convert the tape to a DVD.

The way Lois had demanded she throw the tape away had rankled for some reason, like Lois had been trying to hide something. But that was ridiculous. This deep distrust and suspicion had to stop. Lois obviously had her reasons for getting rid of the tape, and that should be good enough. It wasn't for Jessica to question and definitely not to have the tape converted.

As for Lois's demanding attitude, it only made sense that she was short-tempered with the stress of the flood and all her other duties. She'd at least calmed down for a while once they'd cleared the hurdle of dealing with the church volunteers. Lois had even been smiling and easily chatting as her usual public persona until . . . Reverend Murphy showed up.

Most people who didn't know Lois well wouldn't have noticed, but she had been upset after speaking to him. Jessica had observed the tension in her aunt's face when, right after Reverend Murphy and his friend's arrival, she had approached Jessica to tell her she had to go to her office. It was difficult to speculate on the reason for Lois's sudden change. It could have had something to do with her relationship with her minister or maybe something the other man had said. Jessica had overheard Reverend Murphy mention that the man used to live in this area. Mildly curious, Jessica had asked Lois if she knew the man, but Lois had only said, "Only slightly." And that was that.

Jessica shook her head. What difference did it make anyway? She tossed the tape on the seat, making it bounce off the photo album.

"Hmm." She hadn't taken the time to look at the album yet, so she picked it up. She'd put off her errand this long, what was a few more minutes?

The first photo was of her mom in her Air Force uniform. Jessica pulled it out and checked the back. The date suggested it was around the time she'd been discharged after serving four years. Jessica had always thought it was out of character for her mom, as she remembered her, to choose military service right out of high school. She just seemed to prefer the drifter life: no concerns, no responsibilities . . . not even her own child.

"She's your responsibility, Rachel!"

Jessica's whole body jolted at the memory. She was eight years old, standing on the porch outside Lois's front door. She was supposed to be playing, but instead, she was listening to her mom and aunt argue.

"She is your responsibility, Rachel. You can't just run off and leave her here like a puppy you want to board."

"It won't be for long, Lois. Just give me this, please. I need time to get my head straight."

"You mean time for you to run wild and do Heaven knows what without having to worry about your child? It's the same pattern over and over. Don't expect me to believe things will change now. It's been the same thing ever since . . ."

"Since what?" her mom fired back. "Samuel's accident? Is that what you mean, sister? Can't you even say it? Too much guilt, maybe? Is it too painful to think about that one, big nasty spot on your perfect little life, Lois?"

"Don't you dare go there!" Lois's voice was a sharp, strangled whisper. "Don't even say—" But Jessica's mom wasn't listening. She'd stormed out the front door without even noticing Jessica.

Later that night, after Jessica had gone to bed, her mom came to tell her she was leaving. "It's just for a little while, baby," she said in a fruitless attempt to stem Jessica's tears. "I need to get some things straightened out."

She leaned down to kiss Jessica, the bitter scent of cigarette smoke mingling with overly sweet perfume to fill Jessica's nostrils until she nearly choked, but still she clung to her mothers neck with all her might.

"Just for a little while," her mom repeated as she gently pulled Jessica's arms from around her neck. "Just for a little while, and then I'll come back to get you."

But she never had.

Jessica blinked hard and focused her gaze out the window until the watery sting in her eyes subsided.

She flipped the album page. The next photo was like the one of her dad she carried around, except it had her mom in it too. Her mom appeared happier than Jessica had ever seen her as she smiled up at her dad. He faced the camera, his own smile warm, but more reserved.

She examined the photo for a long time before turning the page once again. She froze at the image of four figures. Her mom and dad were there again, but so was Lois. She stood close to Jessica's parents, and on her other side stood a young man with his arm draped over her. Jessica studied his face. It was the man who had come with Reverend Murphy today! She was sure of it.

What had Lois said when she'd asked about him? That she'd known him only *slightly*? Yet here they were, years ago, holding each other and looking into each other's eyes. Not only that, they stood next to her parents, the four of them all so close together, as if they were good friends.

Dozens of questions raced through Jessica's brain. Why had Lois lied about her relationship with the minister's friend? Had the four young people been as tight as they appeared to be in the photo? It was incredible. All her life, Lois and her mom had been at odds, right up until her mom's death. And, of course, Lois hadn't even let death stop the disdain she'd always shown for Jessica's dad.

She closed the album with a thud, and looked at the videotape again. Whatever was on that tape had something to do with these photos and all of the questions rattling around in her mind. It had to!

Sitting up straight, she put the truck in drive and headed toward the Main Street camera shop.

DREAMS LAST

10

Jessica gazed at the chipped gray paint and worn wooden walls of the roadhouse. The place had probably needed a makeover since before Jessica was born, but the owners, Marty and Barb had never made a single improvement in the six years she had known them. In some ways, the aging façade seemed appropriate, though. If the building were too neat, too clean, too well kept, it wouldn't have been a haven for its patrons. But like them, it was weathered and worse for the wear, so it seemed to welcome and understand them.

When she went to the door, there was a sign that read, "Out for supplies" hanging on it, but that was okay, she still had a spare key. She could wait inside for Marty and Barb to return.

She looked around at the familiar sights: the wooden tables, the bar, and the dusty, vinyl booths. How odd that, after a year of being away, wandering around this old place felt more like coming home than the house where she'd slept and ate for most of her life. It was also oddly familiar to be here for answers, just like the first time she'd walked in the door six years ago.

She'd been thirteen then, but she remembered it as if it had happened a week ago.

One afternoon after school, she marched right in the front door, full of teenage angst and determination. That resolve weakened some as she took in her surroundings. It hadn't occurred to her until she was standing in the middle of the room that this really wasn't the kind of place she should be. This was the kind of place where brawls and shady deals always happened in the movies.

But, before she could backtrack, a tall and slender woman in black jeans and a black tank top entered from the kitchen. She was in her mid-fifties, but her short, dark hair didn't sport any gray. When she saw Jessica, she set down the crate she was carrying and folded her arms with a scowl. "Well, what are you doing? We don't get a lot of kindergartners here."

"Are you the owner?" Jessica asked.

"One of them. Marty Wright's my name. Now that you know that, you should probably forget it and leave." She turned back to her crate, as if that were the end of the discussion.

For some reason, the woman's brusqueness emboldened Jessica. "Are you my grandmother?"

Marty spun around and faced her. "What?"

"I heard some of my teachers talking today. About my dad and his accident, and about how his mom owned this roadhouse."

"Your mom is Rachel Connell?"

Jessica's heart rate picked up. "Yeah. I'm Jess. And your son was Samuel Wright?"

Marty nodded and started unloading glasses from her crate. "But let me tell you something, Jess. Dredging up the past is a bad idea."

"Yes, ma'am. I get that. Really. I don't want to cause trouble. I just want to know."

"Yeah, well—" Marty stopped and looked up as a short, rosy-cheeked woman around the same age as Marty entered the room. "Barb, there you are. We have a visitor. This is Jess Connell. Rachel's daughter."

Barb's eyes widened as she looked at her. "Rachel's daughter?"

The two women exchanged a long look, holding, it seemed, an entire discussion without saying a word. Then, all at once, Barb turned to her again with a welcoming smile. "Well, it's nice to meet you, Jess. I'm Barb Whittaker."

"Um, thanks. Nice to meet you too." Jessica was taken aback. She'd heard the name before, or at least, the last name. Some of the kids in her school liked to play around a deep ravine on the outskirts of town. They unofficially called it "Whittaker's Ravine" after a drunk driver had crashed his car there some ten or fifteen years before. Don Whittaker, the driver, must have been Barb's son.

Jessica refocused on Marty then, wondering if her grandmother was going to kick her out for real this time or actually talk to her about her father.

"You play guitar?" Marty asked abruptly.

"Yes, ma'am."

As it turned out, Marty didn't mention anything about her son that day or hardly ever. Yet from then on, the roadhouse became a kind of second home to Jessica. In the afternoons, before the dinner rush started, she would visit after school. On the nights when the weather was nice enough to sit outdoors, Jessica would play and sing on a makeshift stage outside the roadhouse. She learned songs from all different genres and eras to appeal to the customers. It had been the best thing about her teenage years until…

Jessica squeezed her eyes shut and clenched her fist. The "until" part didn't require much reminiscing; it was still fresh. And Lois had been the cause of it. Just like Lois was the one who'd only ever shared the bare minimum of details about Jessica's parents and their relationship, no matter how much Jessica had pestered her. Even now, for reasons all her own, Lois still seemed to be skating around the truth by lying about the man with Reverend Murphy.

With a frustrated huff, Jessica took out her guitar, which she'd brought with her, and started to play. It was an older KT Tunstall song with a sharp beat that Jessica mimicked by stomping her foot. Before long, she was lost in the rhythm and lyrics.

She'd just finished the song when a dry chuckle came from behind her. "Bad day?"

Jessica whirled around to face Marty, who was leaning against the back door frame and grinning.

"Marty!" Jessica hurried over and stretched up to hug the older woman. It was odd. She didn't hug Marty often, but when she did, it felt like embracing an old friend. Sometimes she almost forgot they were related.

When Barb joined them, there was no need for Jessica to approach her. Barb swooped in and wrapped Jessica in a tight hug. "Just look at you, Jess. You go away for a year and come back looking thirty-seven."

Jessica squeezed her eyes shut and hugged back. "It happens, you know? When I come back for Christmas, I'll probably be ready for Medicare."

Barb lightly thumped her on the back of the head. "Cheeky,

aren't we?"

The three chuckled before settling into a booth with bottles of the grape soda Jessica always drank when she visited. After chatting for a few minutes, Jessica pulled out the picture she'd been looking at earlier and showed it to Marty and Barb.

Marty studied the image. A wistful smile flitted across her face before she pushed it back across the table to Jessica. "It's your mom and your aunt, my Sammy, and Joshua Ridgeway."

"I think I figured that part out, Marty."

She crossed her arms. "Then what is it you want to know?"

Jessica swallowed and looked down at the photo again. What did she want to know? Where did she even begin? She wanted to know something, *anything* about her parents besides the crumbs Lois had thrown her over the years. Did they love each other? Had it really been grief over her dad's death that had made her mom so restless and self-destructive that she couldn't even stay with Jessica?

"I-I just want to know about them," Jessica replied shakily.

Barb reached across the table and squeezed Jessica's hand, but she didn't say anything. Instead, she simply raised an eyebrow at Marty.

Marty took a swig of her soda and set it down again. "Those four? I guess they were just about as close as any friends could be. Sammy and Joshua had played together since they were in rompers. Then, of course, the whole town knew Lois and Joshua were sweethearts, even before they did.

"Sammy and Rachel were close too," Marty mused, twisting her bottle between her fingertips. "But it wasn't like Lois and Joshua, at least I didn't think so. Still, in their senior year of high school, Rachel got it in her head that she and Sammy were meant to be. They said they'd get married when she got out of the Air Force and he finished college. Rachel wasn't my husband, Arnold's first choice as a wife for Sammy, but he reconciled himself to it since she was the only girl Sammy had ever shown interest in."

"What difference did it make?" Jessica asked.

"Arnold was determined Sammy would settle down with the 'right kind of girl' and work for his company once he graduated. He . . ." Marty coughed. "*We* had Sammy's whole life planned out for him. Never really concerned ourselves with what Sammy wanted. But all of that changed that one summer."

When Marty fell silent, Jessica gently prompted, "The summer of the accident?"

"Right. Rachel had only been home for a few weeks when Sammy decided to break it off. No one was expecting that, least of all his father and me. He told us that he didn't want to be married and he didn't want to work for his father. He wanted to pursue his music, wanted to travel."

"How did that go over?"

"Like you might expect. Arnold told him that until he got his head on straight, he didn't need to bother coming around or calling. And me? Being the kind and understanding mother that I was, I told him how disappointed I was in him. And that was it," she finished, her tone tinged with bitterness.

"The next day, he left without telling anyone. On his way out of town, his car crashed and he died."

Jessica's skin chilled, despite the afternoon heat. She stole a glance at Marty's pained expression. "How did you even make it through that? You must have been shattered."

"I was furious!"

Jessica sat up straighter.

"I was furious at everyone and everything," Marty continued. "I blamed Arnold for pushing Sammy away. I even moved out with the intent to divorce him. And I was mad at Sammy for dying out in that ravine."

Jessica felt the little gasp escape before she could stop it. She looked from Marty to Barb. "Whittaker's Ravine?"

Barb met Jessica's eyes, a wary expression in her own as she nodded. "You've guessed right. My son Don was the driver who hit Samuel. Both cars went through the guardrail."

Jessica gulped and stared down at her soda. A deep ache settled in her chest, and when she looked up again, Marty and Barb's faces blurred together in her tears. "You both lost your sons on the same day."

Barb released a sigh and pressed a tissue into Jessica's hand. "Sweet girl," she murmured. "Sweet, tenderhearted girl."

Jessica wiped her eyes and gestured at her face. "I'm sorry about this. Marty, please go on . . . if you want to, I mean."

Marty gave her a small, affectionate smile. "As I said, I was angry at everyone. And I even took it into my head to be mad at Barb here, just because she was Don's mother."

Jessica's lips parted.

"Yeah, I know. I was in a sorry state," Marty grumbled then looked at Barb. "One day, I marched over here, ready to let Barb have a piece of my mind."

"That was a rough day." Barb picked up the story. "The business was in bad shape. The building was falling down around my ears."

Jessica raised a brow and looked around the room.

"Don't say a word!" Barb raised a finger, but her tiny grin belied the imposing gesture. "I know it doesn't look like much now, but believe me, it was worse then."

Barb's face sobered. "My accountant had just been here telling me the best thing would be to sell and cut my losses. On his good days, my boy Don had been a real help with the business. Most people didn't know that. H-he had a good head on his shoulders, but he struggled. So anyway, I'm sitting alone, a blubbering mess over everything, when Marty storms in here like a sheriff in a western movie."

Despite the serious topic, Jessica couldn't help but smile. She could definitely picture that.

"I braced myself," Barb continued. "I could guess how she felt, and I knew all the terrible things the whole town had been saying about my son."

Marty's expression went uncharacteristically soft as she gazed at Barb. "When I saw how upset and exhausted Barb was . . . I don't know; my anger just kind of seeped away. I knew I was looking in a mirror, looking at someone, the only one in this situation, who was every bit as broken as I was. We ended up talking for hours."

Barb chuckled. "The next thing I know, she's giving me business advice."

Marty shrugged. "I did a lot for Arnold's business when we were first starting out. I had a few ideas to keep this place going. Then when Arnold died a year later—we'd never actually divorced—I sold the business and became a full partner in the roadhouse."

Jessica nodded and drummed her fingers on the table. "It sure sounds like a big shift from the life you had before, Marty. But I guess there was no going back to that anyway."

"You're right," Marty agreed. "When I lost Sammy, everything changed. It wasn't just the grief, though." She leaned forward. "You still read your Bible?"

Jessica blinked at the abrupt question. "Yes."

"Do you remember all the Old Testament stories about idols and graven images and how it always seemed to bring downfall?"

Jessica nodded.

"Hmm, that's sort of how my life had turned out. Arnold and I weren't born well off. We grew up on the wrong side of the tracks, but we worked hard to get on the right side. Once we did, well, it seemed like the lifestyle was all that mattered to us: having the right house, socializing with the right people, getting more and more things until everyone forgot where we'd come from. That drive became an idol."

Marty drew a shaky breath. "It was an idol, and we were willing to sacrifice my son to it: his dreams and who he was."

Jessica pursed her lips. "So after Samuel died, you walked away from all of it?"

"That's right. I had to get away. Had to throw it all away and do something more worthwhile. No, Barb and I aren't exactly a couple of Mother Theresa clones over here, but we try to be here for the people in this town with food and company, if nothing else."

"You've definitely done that," Jessica murmured, her mind journeying back through the memories again. Coming here had been like gaining not one, but two eccentric grandmas. More times than she could count, she had poured out her troubles to Marty and Barb and lost herself in her music. No matter how her day had gone, she always walked away comforted. "You've done all of that and more."

DREAMS LAST

52

11

Lois struggled to make small talk with the ladies in her pew and forced herself not to check her watch again. She didn't have time for it, but she had to be here.

Earlier that morning, the church email blast had informed members that some of the buildings at "The Farm," a property the church owned outside of town, had been damaged in the recent storm. Although the buildings were only used for youth activities and retreats, none of which were scheduled any time soon, church leadership was eager to start repairs right away. The email had asked for volunteers to help with the effort.

There were a half dozen other things Lois could have been doing other than showing up for this volunteer meeting, but she didn't have a choice. This was her chance to pay the church back for the help they'd given her.

Thanks to Jessica's persuasion, she'd agreed to accept free labor to clean up her house, but thoughts of merely ending the matter with a feeble "thank you" felt like a nest of church mice scampering under her skin. She'd needed to find a way to balance this scale that had left her indebted to so many people. The email had presented the perfect opportunity, if only the rest of the group would get a move on!

As if taking pity on her internal fuming, Doris, the woman organizing volunteers for the day, stood up in front of the group and began handing out assignments.

"Okay, friends," Doris swept her grandmotherly smile around

the room. "First off, would anyone like to help—"

To avoid wasting any more time, Lois raised her hand before Doris even finished.

The older woman blinked twice. "Well! Someone has a servant's heart this morning! Okay, Lois, you can give Mr. Ridgeway a hand collecting lumber and supplies from storage."

"Uh . . ." Help Joshua? Lois had to get out of this now.

Joshua picked that moment to enter the room. The way his attention immediately focused on Lois made her skin tingle hopelessly.

"Good news, Mr. Ridgeway, Lois has already agreed to help you collect supplies," Doris chirped.

Too late to run now.

Several of the older members in the group—probably the ones who remembered Lois and Joshua from when they were kids—seemed to be snickering and nudging each other.

Lois's face heated. Great. Now there would be rumors.

Doing her best to ignore the rest of the room, Lois stood and nodded to Joshua. "Shall we?" She turned and left the room without waiting for a response.

****

Lois stood back as Joshua opened the passenger door of his truck for her then climbed inside.

Joshua got in the driver's seat and slammed the door. A jolt traveled down Lois's spine as her mind filled with the sudden image of herself sliding over to snuggle beside Joshua, the way she had countless times when they were young. Even now, she could close her eyes and recapture the ineffable warm, safe sensation she'd get whenever she was pressed against him.

Her eyes flew open. No, no, no. She could not allow her treacherous memory to hijack her thoughts like this! There were twenty years and miles of life between then and now.

She snuck a sideward glance at Joshua. His brow was lowered in a scowl and his mouth set in a firm line. It was highly unlikely that any tender memories were running through *his* brain at the moment.

But that assurance did little to lift the curtain of awkwardness that enveloped them. Desperate to escape its oppressive weight, Lois spoke first. "So, where do you live now?"

That's it. Stay in the present day at all costs.

Joshua ran a hand over the light stubble sprinkling his chin. "Now? That's hard to say . . . that is, I've been in Chicago the last several years."

"Urban life, huh? What do you do there?"

"I'm a high school teacher."

Lois twisted to face him in surprise. "You are? Is that what you've been doing this whole time?"

He ran a hand through his hair. "I've been teaching for around fifteen years. I had to get more school for the certifications. Before that, I just did a little bit of everything, I guess."

Lois watched out the window. The same old street signs and buildings they always used to pass zipped by her view. "Do you enjoy teaching?"

"Yes. Never a dull moment."

Lois frowned. A scripted response.

They drove in silence for a while. When Joshua spoke again, his tone was more natural, as if he'd remembered whom he was talking to. "It's pretty great, actually. Not one of my students has been exactly like the other, yet, you come to see categories, or types, you might say.

"They're all shockingly bright, Lois, each in his or her own way. After a while, you get to know them. There are the serious, dedicated students, the ones who could stand up and teach the class better than I do. Then there are the ones that put all their intelligence into sarcasm or practical jokes. I can't possibly relate to them, you know."

He sent her a wry grin—the first she'd seen from him since this bizarre reunion started—and her breath stuttered, but she managed to return it. "No, of course not, *you* don't have a mischievous bone in your body."

Joshua chuckled before continuing. "Then there are the ones who are smart. Really smart with a whole world of potential, but for one reason or another, no one has ever showed them. Watching them grow and figure out how to enjoy learning and discover all they can do . . . it's amazing. I never get tired of it. It's enough to make up for all the frustrations of getting to that point."

"Wow." It was all Lois could think to say. It was all she needed to say, though, because now that he'd gotten started, Joshua seemed happy to keep talking about his students, past and present, for several more minutes. His face seemed to brighten with an inner light as he spoke.

And she listened in quiet astonishment. The Joshua she had known had been full of ambition for a business career. Specifically, he'd wanted to start his own company and run it using more up to date practices than his father had. When they were in college, it had been all he'd talked about, to the point that she'd worried it was an obsession. Spending his life, not only teaching, but actually investing himself in his students was something she never would have expected.

Strangely, these changes in Joshua seemed to do more than anything to ease the awkwardness. It was almost possible to imagine she was riding next to a completely different person, a new acquaintance, maybe. Maybe they could get to know each other and be civil here in the present, leaving the past where it belonged. It was more than she deserved, but she hoped for it nonetheless.

When they arrived at the Farm, she and Joshua fell into a comfortable rhythm of unloading and organizing the paint, wood, tools, and other building supplies. Not long after that, the other volunteers arrived, and the group worked for several hours repairing the damaged parts of the buildings and clearing away debris.

Lois and Joshua were quiet for the first part of the drive back to town until Joshua turned and said, "City Manager, huh?"

"Yeah, for a couple of years now."

He nodded slowly. "You must be really good at it. I've only been in town a week or so, but I've already heard a lot of people talk about you. They really respect you, Lois."

Their eyes met, and a sober smile passed over his face.

Respect. He was one of the few people who knew how much that mattered to her. It was probably one of the only things that mattered in her life. Did he suspect that too? Did he think that little fact was as pathetic as she did at the moment?

He faced the road again and his jaw firmed. "You know, that's what I wanted for you too, don't you? I wanted to make sure people always respected you when we got married."

Lois flinched. "Joshua . . ."

"No, Lois, please listen. I wanted to talk to you about what happened. I wanted to explain."

The hand she held up to stop him shook a little, but her voice was firm, as she said, "No, you don't need to explain. I know what happened, but it was twenty years ago. A lot has happened. We've moved on. I don't think . . . I don't want to talk about this. Let's just focus on today, please. Hmm?"

Joshua glanced at her and remained silent. Finally, he heaved a sigh. "All right, if that's what you want. I'm sorry. I didn't mean to make you uncomfortable."

They didn't converse anymore during the drive or even when they got to the storage facility and unloaded the materials that were left from the day's work.

Lois did her share of carrying and stacking, her mind struggling to unravel Joshua's desire to talk.

Talk about what? His going away all those years ago? They both knew it had been his natural response to what she had done to him. Action and reaction. There was an icy elegance in the balance of it all. But that didn't mean she wanted to discuss it.

Once the truck's bed was empty again, they started to get back in the cab, but Joshua stopped short of opening her door, his hand fixed on the handle. Lois winced. *Please don't bring it up again.* When she looked up to study his face, though, he wasn't looking at her. He was looking at the building next to the storage units, which was separated by a short chain link fence.

The roadhouse.

A heavyset biker type in his sixties stood on the roadhouse's back deck emptying a trashcan and talking to a tall, broad-shouldered black man who was just a few years younger than his companion. Lois seemed to recall that Marty called them "assistant managers," but Lois had always suspected "bouncers" would be a better term for the two rough-looking men.

Their conversation grew more animated when they were joined by a third person.

Lois gritted her teeth once she realized who it was. "That girl," she muttered.

"Is something wrong, Lois?" Joshua turned to her in concern. Then he followed her gaze. "Hey, isn't that your niece?"

Lois only nodded as she began to eavesdrop on the conversation happening on the other side of the fence.

"Jess, you gotta play something for us. It's been a whole year!" the biker was saying. "How about some Jewel, huh?"

The black man crossed his arms. "Curly, you always want to

hear Jewel, man. What is it with you?"

"Hey! You gotta problem with good music?" Curly punched his friend in the arm. "I guess you do. Last time I was in your car, Baker, I saw a disco CD!"

"You did not! It was—"

"Guys, guys, time out," Jessica managed to interrupt despite the fact she was laughing. "I'll play, okay?"

The two men grinned and sat down on a picnic table bench. Jessica bent down to pull her guitar from its case then took a seat on a bench facing them.

She thoughtfully plucked a few strings then started playing the intro to Jewel's "You Were Meant for Me." Lois recognized it instantly since it had been pretty popular when she was a teenager.

Jessica played and sang the song with simple sincerity, like she was making music to see two old friends happy and not performing for a crowd.

"She's really good," Joshua remarked.

Slowly, Lois's irritation with the girl faded as she closed her eyes and drank in the melody and melancholy lyrics about life after a breakup. The sadness pulled her deep into her own recollections.

After Joshua had left, she'd worked to accept that he wasn't coming back. But in some desperate corner of her soul, she'd hoped he would. Joshua had been one of the very few people to ever show her real love. She'd hoped that love was big enough to forgive and let them move on. She'd clung to that hope until she couldn't cling anymore. At long last, she'd come to terms with the fact that the dreams of the life they'd build together were shattered.

Ever since then, she'd worked on building her own life, and she'd accepted the balance. Embraced the action and reaction without complaint. But here, in the bright sun, standing beside Joshua and listening to Jessica's sonorous voice sing the refrain, "Dreams last for so long," Lois also accepted the fact that, in the life she'd taken so much pride in building, she was only half alive. There was no sign of the loving, laughter-filled home she'd longed to have. No sign of the man she'd once given her heart to. She rarely took the opportunity to dwell on that pain, but now, she breathed in every ragged particle of it until it scraped her lungs and bruised her heart all over again.

"Joshua . . ." She opened her eyes as she spoke and nearly gasped to find him staring straight at her. His expression was sorrowful and soft, nearly to the point of tenderness.

"Yeah?" He took a step closer.

Her heart rate sped up. Any closer and they would be touching.

But Jessica's song ended then, and Curly and Baker's noisy applause shattered the moment.

Gradually, Lois's heart regained its usual rhythm. "I'd like you to take me back to the church now, please."

DREAMS LAST

12

When Jessica got back to the house after leaving Marty and Barb, none of the inside lights were on even though Lois's car was in the driveway.

She went to the living room and found Lois sitting in her favorite wing back chair, eyes fixed on the rug in front of her. Lois didn't look up as Jessica entered. Despite the fading light, the dark circles under Lois's eyes were evident. But for the fact that Jessica had never seen Lois shed a tear in all the years she'd known her, she would say her aunt had been crying.

"Aunt Lois?" Jessica called softly.

When Lois looked up, there was unmistakable pain in her eyes.

Concern swirled through Jessica's stomach as she settled on the sofa next to Lois's chair. "Aunt Lois, what's wrong?"

Lois's attention focused on Jessica. Her tone was shaky and vulnerable, for once. "Sometimes, it just feels . . ."

Lois stopped then blinked hard. "It's nothing. I'm just tired. Today was a long day. The church was doing cleanup out at the Farm, and I helped with that. I guess I'm just not used to doing much physical labor anymore."

Jessica released a gentle laugh. "You could have called me. I would have been glad to help too."

"I doubt you would have had time, with all you're doing." Lois's expression hardened a fraction. "Including finding your way back to the roadhouse again."

Jessica's spine stiffened. It wasn't what Lois had said that made the observation sound so caustic; it was the way she'd said it, with the word "roadhouse" dripping with derision.

Mentally, Jessica counted to ten before coolly responding, "I did go there, yes. I wanted to see Marty and Barb while I'm in town."

Lois sniffed. "Nice to see that building your career in the big city hasn't made you cautious about who you associate with yet."

"What difference does it make who I hang out with now?" Jessica retorted, her hands clenching. "I'm not your problem anymore. I don't live here. As soon as this mess gets sorted out, I'm leaving."

Lois's head snapped back and she drew in a sharp breath, but Jessica pressed on. "Just a few more days and your precious reputation will be safe."

"You are so ungrateful," Lois seethed, eyes narrowing. "What do you know about reputation? Your classmates never laughed at you when your dad showed up an hour late to get you from school, so drunk you were scared to get in the car with him. The old ladies in town didn't cluck their tongues about what a shame it was you had to grow up in such a terrible house. No one talked about you behind your back because of me. I worked for their respect and you could have had it too, but instead you tried to sabotage it at every turn by going to places like the roadhouse. Four years! Four years you snuck over there without telling me. You have no concept of what reputation really means."

"Not for lack of trying on your part," Jessica replied quietly, taken aback by the revelations in Lois's tirade, but not completely silenced. "Look, I see why respect matters to you so much, but you have to understand. My going to the roadhouse was not a personal attack against you or what you stand for. I went there because my music was appreciated, yes, but also because I felt like I found comfort and warmth there for the first time since Mom left. Marty and Barb helped me through those nightmare weeks after my best friend died. And they were there when I found out Mom had died too. Sure, she'd ditched me, but it still hurt to lose her for good.

"I thought maybe you could understand that. But no. When you realized I'd been going there all that time, you forbid me to go back with barely an explanation except for how it hurt your reputation!"

Jessica's head throbbed with the memory of a previous shouting match. *Playing music for a bunch of lowlifes and drunks! How could you humiliate me like that?"* Lois had screamed. It had been the only time she'd ever heard her aunt lose control like that.

Returning to the present, Jessica shook her head. "I couldn't understand how going to the one place I could make sense out of life was such a crime."

"So you decided to get payback?" Lois demanded.

"Payback?" Jessica asked in surprise. "What do you mean?"

"You left."

"I'd been planning to move to Florida for ages. You knew that," Jessica pointed out.

"Yeah, you were planning to go live with your mom, but she died and you went away anyway. You took off without explaining how you intended to get down there, and you didn't call along the way or when you arrived. You didn't even call when you decided to move to New York either. You just clammed up!" Lois's voice shook the tiniest bit. "And now? All you ever do is email every once in a while or call when you know I won't be available to answer."

Jessica's stomach knotted. "I-I didn't know it would bother you that much."

Lois's eyes widened with incredulity, but she didn't respond.

"Aunt Lois, seriously. I—"

"Let's just forget about it, okay? I'm way too tired to continue this tonight."

Without another word, Lois stood and walked, first out of the room and then out the front door.

****

A few minutes after Lois left, Jessica shuffled out of the house, arms and legs still shaky from the argument. Obviously, her body didn't enjoy confrontation any more than her mind did. She wasn't used to conflict with anyone, really. Up until a year ago, she'd never quarreled with Lois. Not that she hadn't had her issues with her aunt over the years, and vice versa, but it hadn't been enough to spill over into angry words until the day Lois had discovered Jessica had been going to the roadhouse.

As nasty as that day had been, in some ways, today had been even worse: so raw and unexpected. Was this just the way their relationship would be now that she was older? If that were the case, it was probably a good thing she was leaving again, and it was best she didn't plan too many visits in the near future.

That would likely make Lois happy, at least.

Or maybe not.

Jessica halted and leaned against the wall of the house. In her head, she replayed the part of the conversation where she'd told Lois she would be leaving soon. In that instant, her aunt had looked anything but happy.

Maybe . . .

Jessica's phone started buzzing in the back pocket of her jeans. Giving her head a shake, she grabbed the phone and checked the caller ID.

Forcing her voice to sound upbeat, she answered, "Hey, boss. Did you get my email?"

"Yep!" Clifton chirped. "I don't know how you had time for all this."

"I worked on the files last night. As you know, there's not a lot to do around here after dark. Nothing advisable, anyway."

Clifton chuckled. "Well, you saved me a lot of work, so thank you. And what's this about you wanting to take that computer course? It's a night class, right?"

"Yeah, an online course. If I can learn this new program, I can organize your client files even faster."

"That sounds great, if you want to put in the time to learn it. I just don't want it to eat up into your music schedule too much."

The stone that had formed in her stomach ever since that failed audition settled deeper at Clifton's words. "I don't think that will be a problem," she mumbled.

Clifton went quiet. He was contemplating an argument, maybe. Finally, he said, "Oh well, you have a few weeks to decide yet. Anyway, how are things there?"

She paused a second too long before replying with a strained, "Fine."

"That bad, huh?" he said knowingly.

Ugh. Why was she so bad at hiding her feelings sometimes? "I wouldn't say bad, no. Mostly, things have gone smoothly. It's just that my aunt and I still have our issues."

She gave him a vague overview of their argument before concluding, "None of it was anything new, though, except for her being so upset about the way I left and not checking in more. I honestly didn't think it would bother her." Her breath escaped in a dejected *Whoosh*. "Was I just being childish?"

"Oh, I don't think so. Or if you were, it was only in the sense that you couldn't understand what it's like to be in charge of another person."

Jessica frowned at the phone. "What do you mean?"

"What I mean is, parenthood, guardianship, whatever you want to call it: it's tough, and worrying is a big part of the game. You spend time thinking about all the bad that's out there in the world, and it's scary."

His tone sobered. "Sometimes I think I should have worried more. Maybe then, I wouldn't have lost my little girl."

"Clifton, that wasn't your fault." Jessica squeezed her eyes shut. "She wouldn't have blamed you. You have to know that."

"I know, and thank you. I guess I'm just trying to say that, while I can't pretend to know what your relationship with your aunt is like, I can say that as a parent, those weeks when you left without any information or any calls were probably something like a nightmare for her."

Jessica swallowed. He wasn't exaggerating; just hitting her with the frankness she deserved. And it was starting to sink in. She *had* been childish and thoughtless too.

Probably sensing her need to be alone with her thoughts, Clifton said, "Listen, I'll let you go. But call me if you need anything, okay?"

"Okay. Thank you."

She ended the call and leaned her head against the sun-warmed brick of the house. Had Lois truly been upset when Jessica left? Had she been worried about her?

A tiny spark of joy flickered behind her breastbone, but she immediately quenched it. What was wrong with her? What kind of person finds joy at the thought of worrying their family?

It's just that, for the twelve years Jessica had lived under Lois's roof, she'd always gotten the impression her aunt tolerated her and that she'd only kept Jessica for the sake of family obligation.

Jessica sighed and sat down on the wrought iron bench. It wasn't what Lois had done that made Jessica think she was an obligation. It was what she hadn't done.

Lois had rarely praised, comforted, or embraced her. She'd never shown much feeling around her at all—neither happy nor sad. In short, she'd never done any of the things Jessica remembered and missed most about her mom.

But her mom had left her. When life had gotten too much for her to handle, she had left the care of her own daughter to someone else. Lois, on the other hand, had given her a home and food and security for most of her childhood.

Which one had really shown her love?

Jessica mulled over the question, tracing a crack in the sidewalk with the toe of her shoe. A mild breeze sifted the blades of grass in the front yard and carried the sounds of distant traffic, along with an answer. Maybe both women had shown love, as they were able.

Looking up at the cloudless sky, Jessica sighed again. "Love. Sometimes we really make it complicated down here, don't we?"

13

As soon as she walked away from the taxing discussion with Jessica, Lois got in her Buick with the intention of driving straight to the roadhouse. She didn't have a clear notion of what she wanted to say to Marty and Barb, though; her mind was still too muddled.

I didn't know it would bother you that much.

Jessica was too genuine to feign the wide-eyed astonishment in her green eyes when she'd realized, apparently for the first time, that her leaving had upset Lois. The girl had truly thought Lois would be unfazed to see her—an inexperienced seventeen year old—take off halfway across the country with few plans or resources.

Lois gripped her steering wheel at the memory.

The first few days after Jessica left, Lois kept her phone close at all times, while she waited for updates. She tried her best not to dwell on the stories she'd heard over the years about young female hitchhikers who were murdered or kidnapped. By the time Jessica finally did call to tell her she'd arrived in Florida, Lois was all wound up inside. But somehow, her great relief at knowing Jessica was safe had translated to temper, and she'd snapped at her niece.

It shouldn't have been surprising that Jessica had interpreted Lois's response as indifference. No, this wasn't *surprise* causing pressure to expand in Lois's chest like a bad case of heartburn.

How could Lois be surprised? The whole reason Jessica had left was because she'd felt Lois had cut off her only comfort by forbidding her to go to that stupid roadhouse.

That roadhouse! Lois fumed and pressed the gas pedal harder.

A lot of this mess wouldn't have even happened if it weren't for Marty Wright. Lois had nearly said so to Marty's face a year ago, but the conversation had derailed. Well, not this time! This time, she wouldn't let Marty turn the focus on Lois's issues. She wouldn't let—

Lois eased off the accelerator. She'd barely made it out of her neighborhood, but second thoughts were starting to catch up, along with the memory of that last confrontation. She groaned and pulled off the road into an empty parking lot.

The night after Jessica ran away, Lois went to the roadhouse shortly after it closed. When her furious knocking didn't bring an immediate response, she marched to a partially open window and shouted Marty's name.

Once Marty opened the door and led Lois inside the empty, half-lit building, Lois turned on her. "What gave you the right to corrupt my niece? You and Barb and this tacky wasteland! Was it revenge? Were you finally settling your score? Do you really want to tangle with me? I pulled strings for you, you know? Made sure nobody closed this place down over any of the code violations you doubtless have. But I can easily reverse course, if I want. How did you never think of that all these years when you let Jessica hang around here?"

Marty had met her tirade with an exasperatingly casual shrug. "The child needed someplace to go. She needed a grandmother."

"You're not even—"

"What difference does it make?" Marty cut her off. "Family is about what you do, not just who you shares your blood. It's about being there when you're needed most. And that's what I was trying to do. It had nothing to do with revenge. I don't know why you think that."

"Because you blamed me for Samuel! I know it. Everyone did: you, Joshua . . . Rachel." Lois's voice weakened as she said her sister's name.

"Rachel, yes," Marty murmured, turning sharp, searching eyes on her. "Did she blame you until the end? Jess said she didn't think you had any feeling at all about your sister dying. But that's not the problem, is it? You won't let yourself grieve because you don't think you have the right."

"You don't know what you're talking about!" Lois exploded.

"I know about driving away someone you love only to lose them for good," Marty said, her dark eyes flashing with sudden pain.

"Stop it!" The sorrow Lois had tried so hard to keep at arm's length burrowed closer.

Marty stepped closer. "I know what it's like to realize you'll never have the chance to make things right."

"Why are you doing this?" Lois whimpered, and before she knew what was happening, she was sobbing uncontrollably.

She plopped onto a chair, rested her elbows on the table, and buried her head in her hands.

After a moment, she heard a thump on the tabletop and looked up to see a glass of clear liquid sitting in front of her.

"No, I'm not here to numb my brain like everyone else around this place!"

Marty sighed. "Will you relax? It's not booze. It's club soda for your stomach."

Lois glared at her through blurry eyes, and Marty gave another one of her trademark shrugs. "If you're about to spill a couple of decade's worth of pent-up grief, you're bound to get a little queasy."

Lois *had* been queasy. But after drinking a sip of the club soda, she was also mortified at herself for having such a massive breakdown. Setting the glass down with a thud, she shot to her feet and all but ran out of the building.

As Lois blinked away the memory, she looked around at the empty parking lot, noticing it was almost dark.

What was she doing? What was the point of going back to the roadhouse for another pathetic scene? And it *would* be pathetic because there was no getting the upper hand with Marty.

Things had been so different when Lois was growing up. When she and Joshua would go to Marty and her husband's house to see Samuel, Marty was always kind to her. She'd been one of the few adults who hadn't pitied her. But that was then. Now that Lois had the trust and admiration of everyone else in town, Marty seemed to feel the opposite. She could always see right through Lois.

Lois wasn't sure which was more pathetic: the fact that she'd chosen Marty, of all people, to witness her hysterics that night, or the fact that, for almost twenty years, there had been no one else in her life she could be that open with.

14

Jessica looked up from her guitar and frowned when the front doorbell rang. It had been less than an hour since Lois had driven off. Was she back now? Had she forgotten her house keys?

She opened the door to find Joshua Ridgeway standing on the porch.

He smiled at her. "Hi. Is Lois home?"

"No, she went for a drive, I think. Do you want to leave a message?"

"I just wanted to give her this." He reached in his pocket and pulled out a cellphone. "She left it in my truck when we were out helping with the Farm today. Can I just leave it with you?"

Jessica accepted the phone with an incredulous grunt. Lois must have been really distracted to leave it; she kept her schedule and all her to-do lists on it. "Yeah, I'll give it to her. Thanks."

Joshua started to turn away, but he hesitated. "I guess I haven't really introduced myself yet, have I? I'm Joshua."

She shook his outstretched hand. "Jessica. Nice to meet you. Didn't you used to date my aunt?"

His hand froze and stayed hanging midair even after she pulled her own away. "Y-yes, I did, actually."

It was unfair to ambush the poor guy like that, but it suddenly occurred to her that striking up a conversation with him might be helpful. "You grew up together too, right? I mean, you knew what she was like as a kid?"

He nodded, his smile slipping.

"What was that like?"

"Oh, I don't think I should be the one to tell you about any of that. I'm sure your aunt has shared plenty of stories. But it was nice talking to you." He backed away from the door like a salesman who'd just spotted a Rottweiler in the customer's house, but Jessica followed him outside.

"But she didn't," Jessica said.

"She didn't what?"

"Aunt Lois didn't tell me any stories." Jessica threw up her hands. "Do you understand? I lived with this woman for twelve years and she's practically a stranger to me. Something happened to shut that emotional vault for her before I was even born, and my instinct says that something involves you."

Joshua stopped and looked at her, his face awash with a sadness that tugged at her heart and conscience.

"Look, can we talk about it just a little?" she pressed. "We can sit out here for a minute."

"Okay," he said with resignation.

He sat in the wrought iron chair that matched the bench and she took the bench.

"What do you want to know about?" he asked.

"Her childhood for one. My grandfather was a drinker, right?"

Joshua sighed. "Yeah, he was. For years."

"W-was he ever abusive?" She wasn't positive she wanted to know, but she asked anyway.

"Verbally. But that was bad enough. Your mom Rachel, she took his mean tirades to heart, but not because they were usually directed at her. See, if Lois ever saw their dad yell at Rachel, she'd step in so he'd yell at her instead. But that would make Rachel feel even worse. They always wanted to protect each other."

Jessica's jaw dropped. That was difficult to fathom, given the state of her mom and aunt's relationship, as she'd known it.

"The thing that bothered Lois even more than her dad's temper," Joshua continued, "was the embarrassment. Everyone in town knew about the brawls he'd get into. Sometimes, even when she was little, Lois would have to go find him and walk him home after one of his benders. People gossiped and shook their heads over the situation. What's worse, some of the other kids would ridicule the girls about it."

"But you and my dad were their friends?"

Joshua's gaze dropped to his shoes. "Yeah, we were. Sam was a sensitive kid. He thought the way the others treated Lois and Rachel was unfair, but I didn't think much about it until the second grade. That's when I first really noticed Lois.

"We were learning our multiplication tables and the teacher decided to make a contest out of the drills. You know, where she'd write some problems on the board and have two students race to see who could get them first?"

"Good times," Jessica said flatly.

"Yeah, it wasn't my forte. But anyway, Lois stood up to go against this one guy, Luke, who was probably the meanest and loudest of the bullies. He'd been giving her a hard time on the bus that morning and was even whispering jokes about Lois and her family behind the teacher's back during class. He wanted to psyche her out before the contest.

"Well, you should have seen it. Lois stood up straight and glided up to the board like she was Queen Elizabeth, even with everyone snickering behind her. Then she completely annihilated Luke in the competition. She was lightning fast at her tables, and she could solve two or three problems to his one. The teacher even gave her a few extra problems just to watch her go. Before long, nobody was laughing; we were just kind of watching in awe."

Joshua gave a wry chuckle. "I know I was in awe, at least. So that afternoon, I followed her home and tried to strike up a conversation with her. She told me to get lost, but I couldn't take a hint. It wasn't until we got to her house and I could hear her dad yelling and making a ruckus inside that I figured out she was embarrassed for anyone to see what her home life was like first hand. She turned and gave me this sad, sort of resigned smile and went inside.

"I stood there after she went in for a few minutes, thinking how awful it was that someone like her had to live like that. I made up my mind, right then, that I was going to marry her when we grew up and we'd live in a nice house and always be laughing and happy."

He chuckled and rubbed the back of his head. "I guess that sounds like a silly thing for an eight-year-old to think, but I was 100 percent serious. Of course, I also imagined us eating ice cream and cocoa pebbles for dinner every night. Adulthood was gonna be awesome!"

Jessica laughed. "So how long did it take Aunt Lois to get on board with your idea?"

"A little while. I engaged in the traditional childhood courtship rituals: following her around, passing notes in class . . . valiantly catching her a pet frog from the creek."

"Smooth."

"You'd better believe it. Anyway, she finally realized she wasn't getting rid of me, and we became friends, then later, boyfriend and girlfriend. I like to think she saw that I didn't care about what people said or what her family was like; I only cared about her. We got engaged in college, and it looked like the dream of my eight-year-old heart was going to come true."

"But it didn't," Jessica murmured. Wasn't that how dreams were most of the time?

"No, it didn't," he admitted. "Things happened the summer Sam died. Things I won't tell you about. But his death was the worst part. Rachel, Lois, me: I think we all fell apart in our own ways. I ended up leaving town shortly after the accident. I didn't have it in me to break things off with Lois to her face, so I left in the middle of the night, like a coward, without even saying goodbye."

Jessica drew in a sharp breath. "D-did you contact her later and talk about it? Did you keep up with each other over the years?"

With a shaky voice, Joshua answered, "We hadn't seen each other or even spoken until three days ago."

They sat in silence for a few minutes until Joshua suddenly looked around and stood. "Hey, it's getting late. I better go."

"Okay, yeah." Jessica stood up too. "Thank you for talking with me, Joshua."

He passed her an uneasy smile. "I don't know that it's something to thank me for. I doubt your parents would have wanted you to be burdened with all this drama. Lois probably doesn't either. I imagine that's why she never told you any of it herself."

"Maybe, but sometimes you need answers, you know?"

"Yeah." He patted her shoulder. "Take care of yourself, okay? And take care of Lois too, if you can."

After Joshua left, Jessica remained standing in the driveway, lost in thought. As she began to pace the pavement, her gaze fell on a small puddle where Lois's car had been parked. "Could be transmission fluid," she mumbled absently before resuming her pacing.

Her mind and heart had gone through a labyrinth of emotions and thoughts while Joshua was talking, but the one thought that preoccupied her most at the moment was about Lois and Joshua's breakup. If you could call it a breakup. What had it been like for Lois to have someone she loved and trusted for so many years simply walk out on her?

On top of that, Lois and Jessica's dad had apparently been friends too. She must have grieved his tragic death. Was that the real reason she'd never seemed to like talking about Samuel? Was it too painful?

Grief was so complicated. In some cases, it brought people together, like with Marty and Barb. But in other cases, it drove them apart. It had made Joshua run away and, in some sense, it had driven her mom away too. The more Jessica heard, the more it was beginning to look like her mom's problems had started with Samuel's death.

Jessica's breath stuttered.

Her mom hadn't just walked out on her when she'd left years ago; she'd walked out on Lois too. How had Jessica never seen that? Her mom had been Lois's only family. At one point, according to Joshua, they'd been close sisters. Yet she'd abandoned that connection.

"Oh, no," Jessica said aloud. She trudged back to the bench and crumbled. "I abandoned Lois too."

Jessica had been so absorbed in her own pain and sense of injury that she hadn't noticed how she had continued the same pattern her mom had started. While no one could fault her for seeking her own life, what Jessica had done went beyond that. By refusing to check in and communicate with Lois after she'd left, Jessica had all but severed her ties with her aunt. And for the third time in her life, Lois had been abandoned by someone she should have been able to count on.

Jessica closed her eyes and didn't bother to wipe away the tears slipping through her eyelashes. "Lord, I'm sorry. Please help me make this right."

DREAMS LAST

15

Lois started her engine and shifted into drive with an exasperated huff. Now that she'd changed her mind about going to the roadhouse, it meant she'd just wasted an hour on aimless driving.

Oh, well. At least she'd blown off some steam.

She was just about to pull back onto the road when a truck drove up beside her, blocking her path. Lois blinked and looked closer. It was *her* truck, and Jessica was sitting behind the wheel. Why?

Jessica rolled down her window, so Lois did the same. "Aunt Lois, I would have called you, but you didn't have your phone with you, so I thought I'd take a drive and see if I could spot you." She pointed at Lois's car. "I think you might have a transmission fluid leak. There was a pretty big puddle on the driveway, so it could be urgent."

"Really?" Lois asked in surprise. "D-do you think it will make it back home or should I call a tow truck?"

Jessica glanced at her dash clock. "It might be best to get the tow. It's early enough you can probably still get a truck out tonight. Meanwhile, since I'm here, I can just drive you back home."

It only took a few minutes to get a tow truck on its way, and then Lois was riding shotgun as Jessica drove them home.

"How did you know that about the transmission fluid?" Lois asked.

Jessica smiled. "I've taken a few road trips with Clifton and

Darla, my boss and his wife, you know. When anything goes wrong with the car, Clifton likes to make a point to teach me something about the engine. I've picked up a few things that way."

"I see." From the way Jessica talked about them, it was clear the couple meant a lot to the girl. How many of the recent changes in Jessica were due to their influence? As she'd proven with her frequent visits to the roadhouse, Jessica seemed to have an affinity for forming connections with everyone but her closest family. Lois winced at the bitter tone of her reflections.

"Aunt Lois?" Jessica glanced over at her.

"Hmm?"

Jessica tapped her fingers on the steering wheel and took a deep breath. "I want to apologize for the way I left a year ago and for my behavior since then. I may have tried to make some earlier, but there really was no good excuse for any of it. I was childish and irresponsible not to keep you updated on where I was going and what I planned to do. I shouldn't have caused you unnecessary stress like that."

The girl had kept her eyes on the road all through the apology, but when she finished, just as they were pulling into the driveway, she faced Lois. Her brow furrowed and the tiniest hint of moisture stood in her eyes. "I really am sorry."

Unfamiliar warmth stirred in Lois's heart, rising to form a lump in her throat. "I accept your apology."

****

The days following Jessica's apology were more peaceful than Lois would have ever imagined possible. Since Lois's car was with the mechanic, Jessica drove Lois to work that Friday so she could keep the truck to run errands.

Then they spent the weekend sorting and replacing damaged items together. Lois had thought Jessica seemed efficient when giving updates about her work on the phone, but it didn't compare to the energy and intelligence her niece applied to her work in-person. On Saturday alone, they had finished sorting through a half-dozen boxes, some of which had not even been harmed by the water, but were still in desperate need of organization.

Many of the boxes contained old photographs. To Lois's disbelief, Jessica sorted through them without comment. A younger

Jessica would have spent an entire day making random observations about each photo and trying to wheedle details about Rachel and their family history out of Lois. It seemed, at last, Jessica had come to terms with the fact that Lois had no desire to discuss the past.

It was little short of a blessing that she and Jessica had navigated their conflict without truly confronting any history. If Jessica continued to leave the past where it belonged, the two of them just might have a shot at a good relationship.

16

Jessica took a big bite of her taco, savoring the fluffy handmade tortilla, spicy meat, cheese, and crispy lettuce. She washed the food down with a sip of her icy bottle of coke. Looking around, it was impossible to suppress a sigh of contentment.

The day was unseasonably mild for a Texas summer. In the tiny park where she'd discovered a world-class taco truck, the shade of the cottonwood trees overhanging her picnic table mitigated the heat from the noonday sun.

Since she and Lois had gotten so much accomplished over the weekend, Jessica had most of Monday to herself to catch up on work for Clifton. The weather was too nice to stay inside, so she'd taken her laptop and searched out an outdoor place to work on her documents for a while.

Jessica finished her meal and returned her focus to her computer screen, but she was soon interrupted by the strum of a guitar. Her heart skipped an excited beat as she glanced around until she spotted the source of the music: an elderly man with graying black hair and a deep tan complexion sitting on a stool beside the truck. He sent her a friendly smile and began to play a lovely, slow melody. She leaned on the table and watched, studying his technique. How many years had he been playing? Probably since he was young, judging by his skill. Whatever the case, it was clear from his expression that music brought him immense joy.

Why do you make music?

When Dorian had asked her that at the audition, she should

have said that music brought her joy. It would have been much simpler and better than dredging up her grief with total strangers. Maybe if she'd left all that in the past, she wouldn't have lost her big opportunity. If the last few days had shown her anything, it was that revisiting old memories could be both painful and inadvisable.

She attempted to refocus on her work, only to get sidetracked once again by an email notification from the camera shop where she'd taken the mini videotape she had found. After all the drama of the past week, she'd almost forgotten about it.

The new, more peaceful turn her relationship had taken with her aunt left her second-guessing her desire to see what was on a tape Lois had been intent on throwing away. But now that she'd gone through the trouble of having the tape converted to a DVD, it seemed a shame not to satisfy her curiosity. It probably wasn't anything important anyway.

****

Once Jessica arrived back at the house with the DVD, she went upstairs to her old room, where she had a small TV and DVD player. She put the disc in the player and sat on the end of her bed.

The screen stayed black for a full minute then, eventually, a fuzzy image of a room appeared. The camera lens shook and adjusted before the picture cleared. From the placement of the window and a familiar old painting of a tree on the wall, Jessica recognized the living room of Lois's house, although the furniture was different from what she had now.

The lens shifted toward the middle of the room, where her dad was sitting on a coffee table holding a guitar. The camera zoomed in on him and stayed.

For the first time, Jessica noticed a time stamp in the corner of the screen. She paused the video and did the math. The video was taken twenty years ago, the month before her dad's accident.

She restarted the playback.

Her dad tuned his guitar for a moment and then began to play.

Even with the first few chords, his fingerpicking skill was impressive as he played a stylized intro to the song "The House of the Rising Sun."

Then he began to sing. His voice was mellow with just the slightest hint of a West Texas twang. Jessica watched transfixed, her eyes starting to burn. For the first time in her life, she was actually hearing her dad's voice! She was hearing him play the guitar just like her mom had told her about so many times. Lois couldn't have possibly realized what was on the tape. Even she wouldn't deliberately keep this from Jessica.

Ignoring the distracting questions swarming through her mind, Jessica concentrated on the video. Something shifted in her dad's demeanor.

"One foot is on the platform
And the other one on the train
I'm going back to New Orleans
To wear that ball and chain ."

He sang the words, his voice soaring in pitch and intensity. He squeezed his eyes shut, and his face mirrored the inner turmoil of the lyrics. Maybe it was instinct or sensitivity, but somehow, Jessica knew he wasn't simply performing the song; he was living it. For whatever reason, he was feeling all of that raw guilt and distress in his heart.

When he finished the song and opened his eyes, there were tears standing in them.

Her dad set down his guitar and looked, not straight at the camera, but above it. Then his gaze shifted to follow the movement of the person recording the video as they left the camera in place and walked around in front of it.

Jessica sat up straight. It was Lois!

Lois put a hand on her dad's jaw. "That was really good, Samuel," she murmured, so low she was barely audible.

He stood up to face Lois, placed his hands on her arms, and rubbed them gently. "Lois, what am I going to do?"

Her hand remained on his face. So tender and comforting. "You know what you have to do."

He closed his eyes and his Adam's apple bobbed as he swallowed. Then his voice lowered to just above a whisper. "It will break your sister's heart."

Lois nodded. "I know, but it's for the best. No good can come from hiding what you really want. Everything is going to be all right."

Then she slid her arms around his neck to embrace him, and he fiercely returned the hug.

The screen went blank again and, a few seconds later, the disc ejected.

Jessica continued to stare at the screen for a long while. Everything inside her turned numb. What had she just watched?

She reviewed the brief conversation.

You know what you have to do.

It will break your sister's heart.

No good can come from hiding what you really want.

Then there was the embrace, the physical contact even before that, the familiarity and intimacy in their interaction.

Jessica jumped off her bed and started to pace her room. No! No, no, no. She absolutely would not allow her mind to go there.

But the thoughts tumbled through her head anyway, one on top of another, with all the unstoppable momentum of an avalanche.

It will break your sister's heart.

He was obviously referring to breaking up with Jessica's mom. When Marty had described it a few days before, she had said that no one was expecting it. But that wasn't true. Lois had known he would do it. This video proved that. She had even encouraged him to do it. Encouraged Samuel to dump her sister! Why would she do that?

Had Lois been that invested in Samuel pursuing his music career?

A harsh, wry laugh almost unrecognizable as her own splintered from Jessica's throat. Lois invested in his music? Lois, who called Jessica's goals pipedreams on a regular basis? Lois, who would always roll her eyes and make it seem like such a hardship when junior high Jessica asked for extra guitar lessons, even though Jessica worked multiple odd jobs to pay her back?

No. Lois couldn't have possibly cared about his music career that much. So the only other explanation for her wanting him to break up with Rachel was that she wanted Samuel for herself.

And apparently, Samuel had wanted Lois too, although he at least seemed to have a conscience about it.

No good can come from hiding what you really want.

They had been hiding their relationship. It made sense. Rachel had been in the Air Force for four years. That was more than enough time for Lois and Samuel to grow close. Fall in love. Maybe even have an affair.

Jessica's stomach swirled faster than a dust devil.

No wonder Lois never wanted to talk about him. And no wonder her mom's life had been such a wreck sometimes. The man she loved had died, but only after breaking her heart, maybe even betraying her with her sister.

Once again, Jessica's thoughts traveled back to the day her mom had left her with Lois. The two women had been arguing. Her mom had brought up her dad. What had she said? *Is it too painful to think about that one, big nasty spot on your perfect little life, Lois?*

She was talking about a betrayal. She must have been. What else could have brought two sisters from a close childhood bond to the bitter, squabbling resentment Jessica had always witnessed between them?

Jessica sank onto the bed. And her mom hadn't been the only one who'd been betrayed. There was Joshua too. He had been extremely vague about the circumstances surrounding his leaving. He'd made it sound like grief over losing his friend had driven him away. But what if the grief had started earlier than that? What if Joshua had found out that his best friend wanted the girl he had loved since childhood? That would be enough to send him running away for good.

Jessica stuck the DVD back in the player and pushed play again. But this time, she wasn't really paying attention. Her head was throbbing too hard.

These past few days, she had come to the conclusion that Samuel's untimely death had sent his friends' lives into a tailspin, but the situation had been more complicated than that. The real tragedy hadn't been a senseless accident. It had been the result of Lois's actions. She'd been the one who—

"What do you think you're doing?" An angry voice crackled through the air behind her.

Jessica turned to see Lois standing in the doorway, her face pale and livid at the same time. She glared, first at Jessica and then at the video playing on the screen.

17

"What are you doing?" Lois demanded for a second time. Not that she needed to ask. When she'd come home and gone upstairs to find Jessica, she'd instantly recognized the music coming from the girl's room. Stepping across the threshold to see the TV screen had only confirmed it. Jessica was watching the video she'd asked her to throw away. The video Lois herself should have destroyed ages ago.

The girl simply wouldn't stop her prying. She even resorted to sneaking around to watch this when she knew full well that Lois hadn't wanted her to.

As Jessica stood to meet her, her face wasn't flushed pink with the expected embarrassment or remorse at being caught meddling. Instead, it was red with fury. Lois took a startled step backward.

"My mom and dad broke up because of you, didn't they?" Jessica seethed, pointing her index finger at Lois. "You and he were having an affair."

Lois's mind went blank. "What?"

Jessica gestured at the screen, now paused on the image of Lois and Samuel embracing. Lois glowered at the TV for a second then rolled her eyes. Oh, boy. Is that what she thought?

"Jessica, that is *not* what was going on there."

"Yeah? Then why did my mom resent you so much? Why did Joshua leave you?"

Lois stomped further into the room and crossed her arms. "What do you know about Joshua?"

"Just that he left town right after my dad died."

"That is none of your business!"

Jessica continued as if she hadn't heard. "Was he hurt because you were running around with his best friend? Was that why my mom was so messed up?"

"Samuel and I were friends! Do you hear me? Friends. He was the closest thing to a brother I ever had. I knew him better than almost anyone. I saw how much talent he had. I saw how miserable and restricted he felt in this stupid town. So I did what you're doing now, and I meddled. I told him to leave and go after what he wanted, even if Rachel didn't fit into that life. I said he needed to be honest with her and with himself."

Lois rubbed her head. "I thought Rachel would make peace with that, if she'd only give herself a chance. I thought she'd love him enough to want him to do what made him happy and to be himself. Instead, when he broke the engagement she'd more or less forced on him, she freaked out. She blamed me for interfering. Started drinking, trying drugs, and anything else she could think of to irk me, including hanging out at the roadhouse every night."

Jessica's face paled as Lois spoke and now she gave a slight gasp and sank onto her bed.

Lois pressed on. "The weeks before Samuel died, Rachel thought she could get back at him too, so she hooked up with some drunken lowlife at the roadhouse: Don Whittaker, Barb's son."

Now, Jessica's eyes were wide and unblinking, a wordless sign that the truth was beginning to dawn on her.

"Samuel and Rachel weren't even intimate, Jessica," Lois rammed home the point. "They weren't like that. Don was your real father. When you were born, Rachel just decided to make up her own reality, one that would make her feel better. So she fed you a load of rubbish about your dad being the gentle, talented, musician we grew up with instead of the irresponsible drunk who ended up killing him!"

Jessica's wide green eyes weren't focused on Lois anymore. Her gaze swept from side to side, as if everything Lois had said were a piece of complicated sheet music written in the air, and she was struggling to read it.

After a minute, she looked up at Lois again. Her expression was wounded and hopelessly lost, but she didn't speak. Then in a blink of an eye, she was on her feet, racing from the room.

As Lois watched her niece vanish, her mind went oddly still, such that every sound was amplified. The clatter and hum of Jessica's ceiling fan. The tick tock of her desk clock. The pounding of Jessica's feet as she ran down the stairs. Finally, the squeak of the front door as it opened and the resounding thud as it shut.

Lois numbly moved to the bed and sat. "What have I done?" she whispered.

Suddenly, the shrill screech of car brakes pierced the air, followed by a dull *thump*.

Lois's heart kicked into overdrive. Her own feet clattered as she sprinted down the stairs and out the door.

Her truck and car were still parked in the driveway, thank goodness. But a quick look around revealed a small crowd gathering on the street in front of the house. Lois elbowed her way through. Her neighbors seemed to back away in slow motion.

A sedan idled in the middle of the road, and lying on the asphalt beside the front bumper was Jessica's motionless body.

DREAMS LAST

18

Lois sat beside Jessica's hospital bed and watched the girl's colorless face. "Doctor, why is she still unconscious? I thought you said she probably only had a mild concussion."

The aging Dr. Nguyen, who'd been serving this hospital for as long as Lois could remember, ambled to the other side of the bed. "It is mild, Lois, but these things can take time. Head injuries can often . . ." He began to drone on about concussions in general and who knows what else, but Lois stopped paying attention.

Jessica, Jessica, please wake up.

It didn't matter that she wouldn't have a clue what to say to her niece when she did wake. Jessica could sit up and yell at her all day, like Lois deserved, if she'd just wake up. Lois reached for Jessica's right hand, but when she once again caught sight of the thick bandage covering it, her own fingers curled into a fist the size of the knot in her stomach.

The doctor was still talking. "And it's a good thing the driver wasn't going too fast when Jessica ran out in front of him. Otherwise, we wouldn't be so fortunate that her worst injury is only her hand."

Lois sat up and glared at the man. "*Only* her hand? Doctor, she's a musician. That guitar is part of her. Not being able to play it would be like losing a limb."

"Now take it easy. That might not happen. We won't know everything until the swelling goes down. There's a chance her hand will be as good as new after therapy. Please, try to relax."

When Lois could only gape at Dr. Nguyen over the absurdity of his last piece of advice, he sighed and sent her a kindly smile. "Well, I'll leave you alone for now. Call the nurse if you need anything."

Lois nodded and went back to watching Jessica.

Even though Jessica's eyes were closed and her unconscious expression unperturbed, it was impossible to banish the mental image of the injured and helpless look she'd worn right after Lois had explained about her real father.

With a strangled groan, Lois slouched deeper into her chair. What was wrong with her? There had to be something damaged deep down inside that would allow her to break the truth to the girl so callously.

As soon as she woke up and recovered, Jessica would probably leave and never look back this time.

A buzzing sound disrupted Lois's increasingly morose reflections, and she glanced up to see Jessica's phone rattling on the table beside her. The name "Darla" appeared on the screen.

Lois hesitated a second then held the phone to her ear. "Hello."

"Um, I was calling for Jessica." The woman's voice on the other side sounded puzzled. "This is her friend Darla."

"Yes, she's told me about you." Lois stood and walked to the hall right outside the doorway. "I'm Lois, her aunt."

"Oh. The aunt." Darla's tone flattened. It wasn't a pleasant response, but Lois didn't have the energy to care why.

"That's right. The reason I'm answering her phone is that I'm afraid sh-she's had an accident."

"What kind of an accident?"

Lois's throat nearly clogged, so she gave a quick cough before explaining about the car hitting Jessica.

"Well, is she going to be okay?" Darla's tone rose in alarm.

"She's still unconscious, but the doctor says it's only a mild concussion. But her hand . . . her right hand is injured. It could be serious. They're not sure yet."

"Oh, no." The fear in Darla's voice fed into her own.

"I'm sorry, but I have to go now. I can text you an update later or tell Jessica to call when she's able."

"Okay, sure. Thanks." Darla ended the call.

Lois turned, re-entered the room, and froze. Jessica was awake now and looking straight at her.

"Jessica!" Lois hurried toward the bed. "How do you feel?"

The girl's brow furrowed, and she stared down at the bandages on her arm. "M-my hand is hurt pretty bad?"

Great. She must have woken up in time to overhear her talking to Darla about it. "It's hurt, but we don't know everything yet. I should go get the doctor since you're awake."

"No, wait. Please," Jessica stopped her. "What happened to me?"

"You were in an accident."

"Oh, yeah. I remember now. I ran out of the house, and there was a car. I guess I was upset after—" Jessica's shoulders jerked, and her gaze darted up to Lois.

Something deep inside Lois shriveled under her regard. She stumbled to the chair. "Jessica, I shouldn't have . . . I could have picked a better way to tell . . . What I said . . ."

Her eyes began to sting, so she closed them. Nothing she could say would undo this. She'd driven Jessica away so many times and, this time, she may have even cost her the ability to make music. She'd given the girl every reason to hate her.

"Aunt Lois, look at me, please." Jessica's tone was gentle and grave, making her sound much older than she was.

Lois swallowed and opened her eyes to meet her niece's.

Jessica gingerly raised her injured arm. "This wasn't your fault, and I don't blame you for it." Then she smiled. *She actually smiled.* "You always warned me to look both ways before I crossed the street."

DREAMS LAST

19

Even with the fuzzy state of her brain when she'd woken up, Jessica had been able to decipher the look of quiet despair on her aunt's face as she talked about what had happened to Jessica. She was worried about Jessica and about her hand not getting better. That thought made Jessica's stomach queasy too.

But the more pressing issue with Lois's demeanor was the obvious guilt she felt over the situation. That, Jessica simply couldn't allow. There was no way Lois should feel responsible for the fact that Jessica had run out of the house like a wild woman and gotten herself hit. It had just been a stupid accident.

In assuring Lois that she didn't blame her, Jessica had hoped to put her aunt's mind at ease. But after Jessica's little quip about crossing the street, Lois was simply watching her with glistening eyes and a hollow expression. That couldn't be good.

"I really mean it, Aunt Lois. I don't want you to feel bad."

Lois swiped at her eyes and sniffed. "Sometimes, I can't believe you and I are related."

Jessica chewed on that for a second before sending Lois a grin. "Please tell me you're not hinting at *another* little family secret, because I think I've heard enough of them for one day. If there are any more, I'll just catch them on the next episode of the *Maury* show."

Lois gaped for a second. Then, a strangled, but genuine laugh escaped her lips. "Jessica!" she chided with a shake of her head.

Jessica's grin grew wider. There, that was better.

After their laughter died down, Lois lifted a trembling hand and gently brushed a strand of Jessica's hair away from her face. "I need to go tell the doctor you're awake."

****

When her doctor and nurses came in to prod and poke and ask questions, Jessica noted, with mild amusement, that Lois asked just as many questions of them as they asked of Jessica. But when they wheeled her back to her room after her x-rays, Lois was nowhere in sight. Jessica didn't mind, though. It was the first quiet moment she'd experienced since waking up in this sterile little room.

She pushed the button to tilt her bed into a half-sitting position and leaned back. Her mind struggled to sort through all the remarks and explanations the doctors had given her, but it was a little jumbled. The main takeaway was they'd need to wait on her x-rays to be sure about how badly her hand was injured.

On any other day, she'd be worried about her recovery, but there were still too many other things to process for her to dwell on that particular concern for very long. Like the fact that she'd just learned who her real father was.

Jessica reached for the water cup on the table beside her and took a long swallow. Something warm and calming like the chamomile tea Darla kept around would've been preferable, but the water brought superficial soothing to her parched throat.

Honestly, it wasn't much of a surprise that her mom would make up a story about Samuel being her dad to make herself feel better. She just hadn't been the type of person who could deal with reality very well. And, when Samuel died, it must have brought her comfort to see Jessica look up to his memory. What would Jessica's childhood have been like if her mom had told her the truth from the beginning?

Jessica's stomach twisted.

Would she have started playing the guitar? Would she have cared about music at all?

Why do you make music?

Yes, why? All her life, she'd been chasing a dream based on a lie. She'd carried around story after story about Samuel, while barely knowing a thing about her real father.

Tap. Tap. Tap.

When Jessica looked up, her jaw went slack. Barb was standing in the doorway.

"Barb! How did you know I was here?"

"You know how news travels in this town." Barb made her way to the chair beside Jessica's bed and sat down. "Marty is still parking the car." Her eyes twinkled. "Naturally, she wouldn't trust that old clunker to the valet."

"Was she afraid he'd sue if the car blew up while he was trying to park it?"

Barb chuckled and shook her finger at Jessica. "No serious injuries to that clever little brain of yours, I see." Her face quickly sobered. "But how are you, really?"

After Jessica described the accident and the extent of her injuries, Barb closed her eyes and shuddered. "My word." She opened her eyes again and leaned down to examine Jessica's hand, tenderly brushing her fingers across the bandage.

While Barb was distracted, Jessica studied the older woman. Was there any resemblance between them? Had her son passed down any of Barb's features? Although Barb's face was fuller than Jessica's, her high forehead and defined cheekbones reminded Jessica of her own. She'd never noticed before. Never had any reason to suspect.

"Lois told me the truth about my mom and Don," Jessica blurted out.

Barb went completely still. After a long pause, she looked up, apprehension filling her eyes.

Jessica's voice went watery. "*You're* my grandmother."

Barb released a long sigh; the tension of the last few moments—or maybe years—seemed to roll off her shoulders. "That's right, sweet girl," she whispered, bending to plant a warm kiss on Jessica's forehead.

Once they'd both recovered somewhat, Barb slowly shook her head. "I'm so sorry, Jess. You deserved a joyous, beautiful beginning, but we didn't give it to you."

"You don't have to apologize for that. And I'm glad to know the truth. So many things are starting to make sense, except . . ."

"Except what?"

Jessica shrugged. "I kinda get why mom pretended Samuel was my dad, but I don't know why she made such a big deal about my taking up music."

"It was guilt." The statement came from the doorway, where

Marty was now standing.

Marty walked all the way in, and Barb turned to face her. They held one of their odd telepathic discussions then Marty approached Jessica's bed. "Well, I hate to see you here, Jess, but I did bring you some fuel."

Marty glanced at the door behind her, as if checking to ensure no staff would come in and object, before presenting Jessica with a large plastic bowl and a spoon.

Jessica opened the bowl's lid and sniffed the rich, meaty aroma. "Monday night stew!"

She stirred the mixture a little but didn't eat yet. "Marty, what did you mean about my mom and guilt?"

Marty expelled a long breath and settled her long, lithe frame on the end of the bed. "Much like Sammy's father and me, Rachel never took his music seriously. After he died, she regretted that. So not only did she make up the story about him being your dad, she also made a point to tell you music was your heritage.

"I know this because she wrote me a letter a few years after Sammy's accident. She told me she was raising you like you were his daughter, and that she'd see to it you carried on with his music dreams."

"Hmm," Jessica mused, absently taking a bite of stew as she digested Marty's words.

Marty settled a determined gaze on her. "The thing is, Jess, I didn't want her to feel guilty. And I'd never want you to feel obligated to somehow fulfill my son's destiny. You don't need to be him or anyone else. 'Cuz you know what? The good Lord made you to be *you*."

She patted Jessica's knee. "And you're enough, just the way you are."

Jessica's face quickly warmed under Marty and Barb's collective regard, but so did her heart. The more she soaked in Marty's words, the higher her spirit soared.

Barb smiled and tapped her on the head. "Finish your stew."

Jessica giggled and ate a heaping spoonful. "Mmm. This is amazing." She paused and looked up again. "You're amazing, both of you."

"You hear that, Marty? We're amazing!" Barb said jovially.

Marty flapped her hand. "Eh. That's probably just the meds talking."

The three of them laughed in the beautiful way loving families do.

20

Lois's footsteps sounded unnaturally heavy in the silent and dim hospital corridor. It was well past ten o'clock, and many of the patients on Jessica's floor were already asleep, judging by the subdued lighting and lack of activity in the rooms she passed. A lone nurse perched behind a computer at the nurse's station. Lois nodded to the woman before pushing on Jessica's partially open door and tiptoeing inside.

She took a startled half-step back when Jessica immediately turned and faced her.

"Aunt Lois, what are you doing here so late?"

Lois responded with a nervous chuckle. "I wanted to check in with a phone call, but I figured you were asleep, so I decided to come by instead."

Jessica's eyes widened. "Oh! Well, that's okay, but you were up here so long already. You've gotta be exhausted."

"Nah, I was too keyed up to sleep," Lois admitted. "How do you feel?"

"I'm a little restless too, honestly. I slept for a bit, but the nurse had to come in and make sure I would wake up normally, because of the concussion thing. So with all that, I guess I'm going kind of stir crazy in here even though it's only been a day."

Jessica chuckled and nodded at the window, where the curtain was half open to reveal the brick wall of the other wing of the hospital. "Not much of a view."

The observation made Lois's spine straighten. "I have an idea."

She hurried to the nurse's station and glanced at the woman's badge. "Hey, Marcia. Do you think it would be okay if I pushed my niece around the halls in her wheelchair for a few minutes? She's feeling cooped up."

Marcia picked up a clipboard and studied it. "Yeah, that should be okay. Just be sure to bring her back right away if she gets tired."

"Thanks."

A few minutes later, Lois was pushing Jessica's chair down the hall and deflecting her questions with a "You'll see" that sounded unusually chipper coming from her.

Lois pressed a button for a set of double doors to open and pushed Jessica into the children's wing. They entered a large unoccupied lounge, and Lois flipped a switch, causing dozens of tiny lights to illuminate on the dark panels of the ceiling.

Jessica gasped. "It looks just like the stars!" She grinned at Lois for a second before looking up again and squealing like a child. "This is the coolest!"

Lois stood back, her own smile a little sad. For all the ugliness Jessica had been through ever since she'd been small, she had managed to hold onto her exuberance. But Lois had rarely given her a chance to show it. She'd been a dutiful aunt, providing the girl with clothing and food and healthcare, but rarely any . . . surprises. How many times had she squandered opportunities to watch a younger Jessica's eyes light up like they were now?

There it was again: her ever-present notion of balance. Lois had been left responsible for her sister's child, and she'd handled her obligations responsibly, providing exactly what was needed, nothing more. What a pitiful way to live. How had it taken her this long to notice?

Jessica was looking at her expectantly now, as if waiting for a response.

Lois blinked several times. "I'm sorry. What did you say?"

"I asked how you knew this room was here?"

"Oh, I saw it shortly after this children's wing opened. I was on a committee to help raise funds for all the remodels and updates, so I got to be one of the first to see it."

"So you basically helped build this? When was that?"

"A couple of years ago."

Jessica shook her head. "I didn't know." She leaned back in her chair and stretched out her legs, continuing to gaze up at the ceiling in silence for a few minutes. Then she added, "Aunt Lois, I'm really sorry about all the times I was so hateful about your reputation. You won't believe me, but I really do get it."

"Get what? My compulsive desire to compensate for past embarrassment by fabricating a phony, picture perfect life?"

Jessica coughed. "Uh, no. That's not what I meant. It's not phony. You're essential to this community. You make things better. You're somebody people can count on and trust. That's what you were building all these years and I—well I never showed much respect for it. And I'm sorry for that."

Lois was pretty well speechless. Was that really what she thought?

"And, while we're on the subject of apologies," Jessica continued, "I'm sorry for yesterday, for accusing you of having a thing with Samuel. That was way out of line."

It was impossible not to marvel at Jessica's candor and sincerity. And how had she grown to be so mature so fast? Here she was apologizing all the time when Lois, the supposedly older, more grownup one hadn't even— "I'm sorry too," Lois spurted, before she could change her mind.

"I'm sorry for the way I told you about your real father. I'm sorry I said hurtful things. And I'm sorry for how I reacted to your suspicions. When I think about it, I can see why you thought what you did about Samuel and me, what with the way your mom and Joshua both resented me."

Lois looked down at the floor. "I take it, when you were talking to Joshua, he didn't explain the real reason he left?"

Jessica tucked her hair behind her ears and rested her elbow on the arm of the wheelchair. "He said he never told you why he was leaving or even that he was."

Lois took a seat in one of the room's only adult-sized chairs. "He didn't have to tell me. I knew. Joshua somehow found out I'd been the one to encourage Samuel to leave town. Samuel's decision to do that cost him his life. How could Joshua and I move on and have a life together after that? How could he ever forgive me?" The slightest of whimpers escaped her throat. "I couldn't even forgive myself."

Long moments passed and neither of them said anymore. The make-believe stars on the ceiling continued to put on a show with all the impassivity of the real heavens.

A metallic creak split the air, nearly making Lois jump.

Jessica was out of her chair and walking closer.

"You shouldn't be walking around much yet. Your equilibrium might still be off because of the concussion. In fact," Lois jerked to her feet, "you probably shouldn't be spending so much time out of your room yet."

Jessica made no move to return to her chair. She met Lois's eyes with frank conviction. "And you shouldn't spend so much time back *there*." She vaguely gestured at the air behind her. Then, without another word, Jessica stepped forward and wrapped her arms around Lois.

For a second, Lois's frame stilled in shock. They'd never been *this* type of family. Why should that change so late in the day?

But as her niece's comforting warmth suffused her, Lois found herself returning the embrace. She shut her eyes. Maybe Jessica had a point. Was anything back *there* more real or more important than what she had right *here*?

21

"You're having surgery on your hand tomorrow? Already?"

Jessica's phone screen was small, but not too small to obscure the astonished expression on Clifton's face as he posed the question while they video chatted. As usual, Darla, who sat beside him, was harder to read, but her eyes widened.

"That's right," Jessica confirmed. "I know it's fast, but the doctor said he might as well get it done while I'm still here in the hospital. He doesn't think it will take long."

"And what exactly is the purpose of the surgery?" Darla asked. "What's the end game, I mean?"

Jessica smirked. "Do you want to know what he said or what the words actually meant?"

Clifton and Darla chuckled as Jessica continued. "Basically, he's repairing damage. If it goes as planned, I should be able to use my hand just as well as I did before. With a little time and some physical therapy, of course."

"And if it doesn't go as planned?" Clifton asked then pursed his lips together, as if he regretted the question already.

With a long exhale, Jessica replied, "If it doesn't, my hand will still be pretty functional, but I probably won't be able to play the guitar again."

The faces on her screen grew grim, and neither spoke for a moment. Finally, Darla quietly asked, "And how are you feeling about that?"

Jessica had been mining her thoughts and feelings all day with the same question. "That's the thing, Darla, I really don't know. I'm not sure if I'm still in some kind of shock, and reality hasn't sunk in yet, or if there's been so much that's happened over the last few days that I can't process it all. Whatever it is, I feel like I'm in a weird state of limbo."

Darla nodded. "Who knows? Maybe that's for the best right now."

Jessica shifted her pillow to prop up her back better. "One thing I do know is that, however the surgery goes, I should still be able to do my job, Clifton. I mean, I can mostly do it now."

Clifton folded his arms and raised his eyebrows. "I've been meaning to ask about that. How are you sending me emails?"

"Oh, it's slow going, but I can type and use my track pad okay with my left hand."

"Okay, I guess the better question would have been: why are you sending me emails? You're in the hospital for crying out loud!"

"They have Wi-Fi here," Jessica said with a shrug. "It gets boring sitting around waiting to be tested or poked on, so it's sort of nice having a distraction."

"I guess I can see that," Clifton conceded. "And I want you to know, whatever happens, you will have a job. More than that, we're both here for you."

Jessica smiled at the screen. There wasn't a doubt in her mind that he meant it. "Thank you."

As Jessica ended the call, a flush of deep gratitude swept over her. It was hard to believe she'd only known the couple for a year. Sometimes she couldn't picture what her life would be like without them. At least there were some things she knew how she felt about.

Her gaze fell to her hand. If she'd been in jeopardy of losing her ability to play guitar a few years ago, she would have been devastated. Music was her life. Had she made an idol of it, the same way Marty had said she'd once made an idol of her perfect life? Maybe she was maturing and broadening her interests, realizing there was more to her existence than some fanciful dream of performing on a stage.

But even as she considered this possibility, she was forced to dismiss it. The days before her audition with the Solstice Riddles, she had been obsessed, *completely obsessed* with nailing it. On some nights, after practicing and watching Riddles' videos for hours, she'd lie awake and imagine what her mom would've thought to see her performing for a big crowd with a successful band.

Maybe the failed audition had been God's way of breaking her obsession, of tearing down her idols—to borrow the Old Testament imagery. And maybe this accident and the resulting injury were too. If so, all that was left for her to do was accept the lesson and try to understand it. Besides, what good had she ever done with her musical gift? She'd only ever used it for her own comfort and to pursue some manufactured dream her mom had left her.

****

The next day, an hour before time to prep for her surgery, Jessica looked up from her laptop to see Curly and Baker from the roadhouse standing in her doorway.

Lois, who was sitting in the corner of the room, jumped to her feet as if about to chase them off but seemed to think better of it. She glanced at Jessica before sitting down again.

Jessica returned her attention to the two men. "Guys! What are you doing here?"

Curly took off his weather-beaten ball cap and stepped in the room. "We're here to wish you luck."

"And to bring supplies!" Baker chimed in. He grinned at Jessica then stepped over to Lois, where he towered over her chair. "Ms. Connell, I figured you'd be too busy helping Jessica get settled to cook the next couple of nights, so I brought you some of my famous fried chicken."

"Famous in his mind, anyway," Curly mumbled.

Baker shot Curly a glare before handing Lois a medium-sized ice chest. Lois's jaw lowered as she accepted it. "Oh, um, wow. This is very generous of you, Mr. Baker."

Marty appeared in the doorway. "I'll say it's generous. We'll probably run short at the dinner rush tonight."

"Oh, Marty, quit your complaining; you know we always have leftovers." That came from Barb, who was, naturally, right behind Marty.

Jessica stole a glance at Lois, who wore a tight smile while her gaze darted around the room as each new visitor appeared. Jessica worked to quell her amusement at Lois's reaction. It was unfair of her. Lois was trying her best to be gracious because of her. Under normal circumstances, Lois would never be found hanging out with the entire staff of the roadhouse.

A buzz of chattering filled the room as the group laughed and talked and shared random stories, but finally, Marty spoke up. "Okay, everyone, I think we should beat it now. The last thing Jess needs is a migraine before her procedure. Baker, how about a prayer before we go?"

"Sure thing," he replied, before bowing his head. The rest of the group followed his lead.

"Father, we thank you for this day and these people and all the things you do for us. And today, we wanna lift up our sister, Jess. We pray for her strength. We pray for her healing. We ask you to guide her surgeon's hands and look with favor on her nurses. Father, Jess has been a light and a blessing to every person in this room. We're grateful for her sweet spirit, and we're asking you to fill her with your grace. In the name of Jesus Christ. Amen."

The "Amen" echoed around the room. Jessica hastily brushed at her eyes then reached out to Baker. His hand dwarfed hers as she squeezed it. "Thank you." She swept a look over the room. "Thank you all."

22

Lois stared down at the ice chest of fried chicken then back up at the man who had brought it. When she'd seen him at the roadhouse and around town, she'd always dismissed him as a rough character who hung out in bars. She'd never dream she'd see him delivering homemade chicken or praying for her niece like a Sunday school teacher. But as she watched him bend down and take Jessica's hand to say goodbye before they all filed out of the room, the truth finally sank in. Jessica was among family.

A lonely, grieving girl had found people who cared about her in the strangest place because she couldn't find it at home. She'd found people who understood her and appreciated her talent. Sure, Jessica had more or less explained all this the day Lois had first discovered she'd been spending time at the roadhouse, and again a few days ago when they'd argued about it for a second time. But, both times, Lois had been too angry to grasp the truth.

Baker and Curly were clearly fond and protective of Jessica. Marty herself had basically admitted to Lois she'd taken the role of surrogate grandmother for the girl. And then there was Barb, who really was Jessica's grandmother. Of course she was attached to her! They shared the same blood. Jessica was a living, breathing connection to the son she'd lost.

Everyday, it was becoming painfully evident that Lois had done the minimum where Jessica was concerned. She'd flattered herself that she'd adhered to her balance, her duty, her obligation. But none of those standards could be applied to a child's life. Children need protection and security, yes, but they also need tenderness and nurturing, two things Lois had failed at miserably. So Jessica had gone where she could find them. And how had Lois responded? She'd yelled at her and told her to never go back.

Of course, Jessica had run away in search of a different life. She'd found new friends to care for her. It wasn't difficult to see how. Baker had been correct in his prayer. Jessica was a light wherever she went, and it had taken Lois all of these years to fully realize it.

"Aunt Lois?"

Lois turned to Jessica, suddenly noticing the room was empty again except for the two of them. "Hmm?"

Jessica's forehead wrinkled. "Are you okay? You seem sort of spaced out."

"I—" Lois shuffled toward the bed. Started to reach out then stopped and drew back. "I need to step out for a minute."

She rushed from the room, leaving a perplexed-looking Jessica behind.

Hurrying down the hall, she found a door to a stairwell and stepped inside. She climbed up one floor and found a small, drab waiting room that was quiet and empty. Inside, she leaned against the wall, trembling.

How did she even begin to process all of her mistakes? All the ways she'd let Jessica down? If she thought about it long enough, she could look back and count all the times she'd pushed her niece's feelings aside, refused to see who she really was, and even tried to ask her to be someone she wasn't. She could remember the way she . . .No!

Lois banged her fist on the chipped wallpaper in front of her. No, this would not help anything. Wallowing in the shame of her mistakes was not the answer. It certainly wouldn't help Jessica.

She could make amends! Because that's what she did. It had taken years, but she'd made up for her dad's irresponsible, embarrassing reputation in this town. And she'd made up for the part she played in Rachel losing Samuel by taking care of her daughter when she'd been unable to. And now, for the ways she'd fallen short with Jessica, she still had a chance to make it up. It wasn't too late. It couldn't be!

She'd be more supportive, encouraging, and attentive. She'd take an interest in the things Jessica cared about.

But as quickly as it had started, Lois's momentum came to a crashing halt.

Jessica cared about her music more than almost anything else. And if the surgery didn't go right today, she could very well lose a large part of that. Regardless of how Jessica had sweetly tried to convince her otherwise, Lois had been partly responsible for this. If Jessica couldn't play guitar anymore, nothing Lois could do would make amends for that.

With a shudder of brokenness, Lois sat down and buried her head in her hands. Desperation drove her to prayer. "Oh, God, please don't take Jessica's playing away from her. Give her a chance to see what she can really do with it. I promise, I'll support her like I should have all along. I'll help her with therapy or specialists or whatever she needs. But please, let her recover."

****

Lois made it back to Jessica's room just in time to see her before an orderly came to transport her to surgery. Then there was nothing to do but wait.

She made a halfhearted attempt at productivity, calling into her office for updates on various matters from her fellow city staff members, but her attention was sorely strained. Only after traipsing down to the cafeteria for a second cup of coffee did she realize over-caffeinating was a mistake. Her pulse was now racing and her nerves were jittery, even more so than they had been before.

Finally, the surgeon came through the automated double doors leading to the operating rooms and approached Lois. Unlike the elderly Dr. Nguyen, Dr. Valdez was high-energy. A smile lit his brown eyes even before he'd fully removed his mask. "Ms. Connell, Jessica did great. Everything went just as close to perfect as I would want it. I'd say with a good six to eight weeks of regular physical therapy, we can have her strumming those guitar strings just like before." He checked the wall clock. "Coming out of anesthesia will take a little while, and we'll want to monitor her to make sure that goes okay, but afterwards, she should be ready to be discharged."

Lois released the breath it seemed like she'd been holding since Jessica was wheeled into surgery. "Doctor, that's amazing! Thank you so much."

He pumped her hand when she offered it and grinned. "I'm gonna go make sure they get the discharge paperwork going, so you can take your little trooper home."

Lois surprised herself by giggling as Dr. Valdez walked away. If she were out here and awake, Jessica would roll her eyes and make some wisecrack about being called "little trooper."

Jessica was going to be okay! She would be able to play again. She could chase after every single one of her crazy, exuberant dreams.

It only took another minute for reality to fully dawn and for relief to release the hours of pent-up tension in an embarrassing gush of tears. Lois grabbed a handful of tissues from a box in the waiting room and rushed toward the nearest staircase before anyone could notice the spectacle.

Down she climbed then hurried across the main lobby and through the revolving front door only to collide with the solid, hopelessly familiar chest of Joshua Ridgeway.

23

They stayed frozen like that for a minute: Joshua's arms wrapped around her and Lois's head buried in his chest. His clean, crisp smell was exactly the same as it had always been. He must be using the same soap he used in college. A more cynical moment might have found her questioning his lack of personal growth, but right now, that fact was simply comforting.

All at once, the absurdity of her situation reared its head, and she pulled back. Joshua dropped his hands. "I-I'm sorry, Lois," he stammered.

Always the gentleman. He was actually apologizing when she was the one who had crashed into him.

"What are you doing here?" she managed to ask.

"I only heard about Jessica's accident today, and I wanted to come over and see if you were both all right." He leaned closer as if suddenly noticing her watery eyes. "Oh, no. Is it serious? Is she—"

"No, no. She's fine. Her hand was injured, but she just got out of surgery and," her breath stuttered out and her vision blurred, "she's going to be just fine."

A wry half-smile played across his lips. "I see. So this is relief."

"Yeah, I guess so." She shook her head and sniffled. "I was just so afraid, and it was so horrible."

Joshua slowly raised his hands to her face and brushed her tears away with his thumbs, as if he did it all the time. "Look, why don't you tell me all about it? If you want, we can run to the cafeteria and grab a coffee."

She all but cackled at the suggestion, a bizarre, unhinged reaction she seemed to have little control over.

With a chuckle, he held up his hands. "Okayyy, so maybe no more caffeine for you, but we can still talk, if you'd like."

Lois bit her lip and turned to look at the windows of the building behind her. "I don't want to leave Jessica alone too long once she's fully awake." She waved a hand toward her face. "But I also don't want her waking up to see me like this."

His expression grew pensive. "I have a feeling she wouldn't mind. But we can sit down with a lemonade or something until you're feeling more composed."

Lois agreed and, a few moments later, they were sitting at a table in the cafeteria sipping watery pink lemonade.

She barely hesitated before telling him the whole story. It wasn't like she had to worry about losing his good opinion by this point. So she explained about the argument with Jessica and the cold way she had told the girl the truth about her father. Then she described the horrible sounds of the accident and the surreal moment when she'd seen her niece lying on the ground unconscious.

"It was like a nightmare, Joshua. For a second, I really thought she was gone. And all I could think was, 'I did this. This is all my fault, just like Samuel.'"

Joshua had been nodding sympathetically through her story until the last part, when he snapped upright. "Like Sam? What are you talking about?"

At first, all Lois could do was stare at him. "What am I talking about? You should know better than anybody! Samuel's accident. His decision to leave town and try to pursue his music. I encouraged him to do it. He was indecisive until I talked him into it. How can you act like you don't understand? We both know that's the reason you left me."

It was Joshua's turn to stare. Then he opened his mouth and closed it again before rubbing his hand over the back of his head. Finally, he scooted forward, while an unexpected intensity shone from his eyes. "Lois, I had no clue that you encouraged Sam. He never told me. The reason I ran out on you and everybody else is because I blamed myself for his accident."

"What? Why?"

Joshua squeezed his eyes shut and took a couple of deep breaths. Then he returned his focus to her. "The night before he left, Sam came over to my place late. He woke me up and said there were some things he needed to talk over with me. It was a nice, clear night so we sat outside. And he told me he didn't want the life he had anymore. He didn't want to marry Rachel. He'd gone along because he didn't want to hurt her, but he'd never really wanted to marry Rachel . . . or anyone else."

Lois pursed her lips and looked away.

Immediately, Joshua's gaze sought hers. "You knew, didn't you?"

She sighed. "I knew that he had a lot of questions, that he was still trying to figure out who he was. All his life, Samuel had been told who he was supposed to be, and never given the space to just *be*."

"Yeah, well, he sure didn't get that space from me that night," Joshua replied bitterly. "I didn't give him time. I didn't listen well. I jumped on a few of the thoughts and feelings he was trying to explain to me and I ripped him apart over them. I asked how he could do this to Rachel or his parents. I asked how he could call himself my friend all those years and then hit me with something like that out of the blue."

Joshua yanked his glasses off and pinched the bridge of his nose. "The choice he was trying to make was eating him up on the inside. I could see it, Lois. Even through all my anger, I could see it, and I didn't care.

"I got my keys and told him I needed to take a drive to clear my head. He grabbed my arm to stop me—to beg me, really—not to leave things like that. And then I punched him. My best friend since before I could remember, I punched him in the face."

Lois swallowed hard. Her air passages felt constricted, like she wouldn't be able to get a full, deep breath no matter how hard she tried. She managed to whisper, "Then what?"

"That was it. I got in my car and drove off, and it was the last time I ever saw or spoke to Sam. Sometime the next afternoon, Marty called and told me he'd been killed."

"Oh my word," Lois whispered.

"That call destroyed me. I mean it completely destroyed me. Sure, I knew I'd lost the friend who was practically my brother, and there should have been grief, but all that I felt was guilt. No, that isn't strong enough. It was condemnation. The first time I looked in the mirror that afternoon, I thought I was looking at a monster."

Lois gasped. "No, you weren't a monster. How could you say that? You reacted badly. You were a terrible friend that one night, but that was one moment in a lifetime of friendship."

Joshua shook his head and leaned toward her. "See, I knew that's exactly what you would have said to me then, but I didn't want to hear it. I knew you'd chew me out for how I'd treated Sam that night, but then reassure me that I'd only made one mistake. You'd tell me that wasn't who I really was; it didn't define me. And I knew I would believe you and eventually move on. But what then? What if, when things got tough, I lashed out at you some day? Or at our children?

"I was afraid and furious at the same time, and I wouldn't let myself face you. I wouldn't accept your comfort, so I ran away like a coward without even leaving you a note. In fact, I told myself it was better that way. Better to make you hate me and forget me."

Lois slumped in her chair, head turned toward the rest of the sparsely populated cafeteria without actually seeing any of the people or hearing the hum of activity. The pulse pounding in her ears was growing loud enough to muffle everything else.

"Better to make me hate you?" she burst out, causing a nurse at a nearby table to turn and look. Face heating, Lois leaned forward and lowered her voice. "I was hurting. I was alone and I was hurting. I grieved and watched my sister's life spin out of control, and I didn't have a soul to turn to. But even in the midst of all that, I never hated you, because I swallowed up the blame myself."

Joshua bent closer. "Lois, please believe me, I would have never dreamed you'd blame yourself. I was so wrapped up in my own stuff back then that I never realized how much Sam confided in you."

"Would that have made any difference?" she seethed. "If you'd known, would you have stuck it out and talked the situation over with me like an adult instead of disappearing for almost twenty years?"

"I don't—" he began nervously.

"Why are you even back here?" she interrupted. "Why are you telling me all this now?"

He raked a shaky hand through his hair. "The real reason I came back was to try to apologize. I wanted to own up to my behavior and make it right, if possible. I know I've hurt you so much, but now I'd like to help you, if I can."

"You want to help me now. Now what? Now that you know you're not a monster? Have you finally decided you can be trusted around people?"

"Yes."

She crossed her arms and scowled. "Oh, really? And when exactly did you figure that out?"

"When Sam forgave me."

Lois's mouth fell open and her arms dropped. His answer had managed to startle her from her anger. Forgiveness from a dead man?

He saw her expression and chuckled dryly. "No, I don't mean anything supernatural. It was something better than that. It was grace."

All at once, that odd, inner light returned to his eyes, the one she'd first noticed a few days ago when he'd talked of his students. "It happened a few years after I left. I'd been drifting, working odd jobs here and there, and never staying in one place for more than a few weeks at a time. I was drinking some too. Basically, I was a mess. Then one day when I was in California, I decided to call my mom for the first time in almost a year. Boy, I'm glad I did for several reasons; one being that she died a few months after that.

"Anyway, she told me Marty Wright had been trying to get an address for me for ages, but my mom had never been able to give her one because I moved around so much. My job in California was going to last for several months, so I told my mom to give Marty my address there. It scared me, honestly. I couldn't imagine what Sam's mom would want to contact me about, but I figured it couldn't be good."

Lois frowned. "Did Marty know about how things ended with you and Sam?"

"I'm not sure. Something in her voice the day she told me about his accident made me think so, but that could've been paranoia on my part."

He scooted back his chair enough to stretch his legs. "I guess I was paranoid about giving her my address too, but I did. Then a week or so after my mom's call, I got an envelope from Marty. Inside was a note saying Sam had left a letter for me in his room before he'd gone away. She'd intended to give it to me, but I'd left too suddenly."

Joshua fell silent, and Lois's curiosity made her impatient.

"Well, what did it say?"

He pulled his wallet from his back pocket. Reaching inside, he retrieved a wrinkled sheet of paper folded over several times and handed it to her.

As she unfolded it, Lois's heart tingled at the familiar sight of Samuel's scrawling script. She could still picture it in the notebook of songs he'd write and show her from time to time.

Josh,

I hit you with a ton of stuff all at once last night. I'm sorry. I know it was a lot to take in, and I should've given you some time to process. If I had, you probably wouldn't have lashed out the way you did. But I know you, brother. That was just a knee jerk reaction, and you'll regret it soon. Maybe you already do. You'll regret it because you're a good man and a good friend. So I wanted to tell you that I forgive you. I can't say it in person because I have to leave. I need to go and figure things out. I don't know what I want where a lot of things are concerned, except that I'd really like to try and make a go of my music.

The next time we see each other, whenever that is, things will be good between us again. I know it. So until then, take care of yourself and take care of Lois. She's really something special.

Your friend,
Sam

Lois blinked away the tears blurring the words of the note and looked up at Joshua, surprised to see moisture standing in his eyes as well. She'd never seen him cry before.

He smiled sheepishly and rubbed his hand over his face. "Sorry, it's just that . . . watching you read it was like reading it for the first time again."

She refolded the letter and handed it back to him. Their fingertips brushed, and a long, searching look passed between them. Then slowly, reluctantly, Joshua pulled back.

"Reading that letter made all the difference," he continued before planting his elbows on the table. "Do you remember Mr. Browning?"

"Our Sunday school teacher?" Lois asked, raising an eyebrow at the abrupt change of topic.

"Right. When we were kids, I spent more time thinking up pranks to play on him than actually listening to his lessons. But in the days after I read Sam's letter, something Browning used to say finally clicked with me: Grace is the thing you'll receive when you need it most and deserve it least.

"Receiving Sam's forgiveness was the first time I knowingly experienced that grace. And I started to change. I began attending a very casual but understanding church. Then I decided to go to school to be a teacher. It was a rough start, but from then on, I determined that I wanted to live in that grace. I wasn't okay with drifting, or just getting by anymore. I wanted to live for grace and learn to show it to others."

He reached his arm out, palm facing up, and pulled up his sleeve to reveal a tattoo on his forearm.

Lois's lips parted. He'd gotten a tattoo? It was words from a Bible verse. "I came that they may have life, and have it abundantly."

"That's what I mean." He gave her a warm smile.

"That's incredible," Lois murmured, partly confused and partly compelled by Joshua's story.

"Like I said," he laughed dryly, "it's been a long, tough process, but a little while back, I felt led to return here. I sensed that I wouldn't be able to move forward or in any other direction until I came back and finally explained all of this to you.

"I know that doesn't make anything better, and it doesn't undo all the pain I've caused you. But I want you to know that I regret it. Hurting you was the last thing in the world I'd ever want to do. And you probably won't believe me at first, but I'd like to try to make it right. I'm here for a while, and if you need anything—anything at all—I'll be here. All you have to do is ask."

No, she shouldn't believe him. Not after all this time. But as she looked into his strong blue eyes, where the intense, energetic youth she remembered fused with the kind, understanding man he was now, she began to suspect that every word he'd spoken was true.

DREAMS LAST

24

Three weeks after her accident, Jessica sat on the living room floor with her back against the sofa, furiously typing up an assignment with her left hand and two of her right fingers. Once she was finished, she attached the document to an email and hit "Send" with a satisfied sigh.

She looked up from her laptop screen as Lois entered the room, carrying two glasses of ice tea. Lois set one glass on the coffee table by Jessica.

"Thanks."

Lois nodded, but she didn't sit right away. Instead, she sipped her tea and watched Jessica. While her aunt's scrutiny didn't unnerve her like it once would, it did stir her curiosity. Lois had been quiet during the drive home from Jessica's afternoon physical therapy appointment and all through dinner.

"Is something wrong?" Jessica finally asked.

"You stopped your PT session early today."

Jessica lowered her eyes. "Yeah, I guess I was tired. It hurt more than usual today, for some reason. Plus, I was ready to get back and finish my assignment for the software class since it's due tomorrow."

"I understand all of that," Lois said slowly, as if choosing her words with care, "but it's going to take all of that effort to get your hand strong enough to play again."

"Maybe I don't want to play again." A tiny chill slithered down her spine as she finally said it out loud.

Lois's lips parted and she dropped into her chair.

"Yeah, I know how that has to sound, coming from me, but I'm serious. I'm already able to work again and take my course. When this brace comes off, I'll be able to do my work even better. What's wrong with that?"

"Nothing is wr—"

"You know what I recently realized, Aunt Lois?" she asked, cutting her aunt off mid-sentence. "This last year, I've been chasing this music dream so hard because it's what my mom would have wanted. Since she's been gone, it's felt like all I've had left of her. But guess what? The whole thing was made up!"

Jessica wildly gestured at her laptop, growing more agitated by the second. "This? This is solid. It's real. I can build a career, a life with this. What kind of life did mom want for me? A traveling songster? Wandering around the country, living in hotels, playing whatever gigs I can, if I'm lucky enough to even get them?"

Her mind wandered back to earlier that day when, against her own better judgment, she had looked up the Solstice Riddles website and seen that they were performing with their former female singer again.

Que será, será. Even if her hand were in good shape, it's not like she'd have any prospects. She'd be back to the audition drawing board. How much thought had her mom really put into Jessica's future?

She brought her good fist down on the coffee table so hard that it rattled her tea glass. "Mom didn't want me to be like Samuel; she wanted me to be like her! Never settling down and running away whenever things get too hard. And if someone needs you, that's just too bad. That can be somebody else's problem. You get to . . . leave." Her voice fractured to a whimper. "You get to leave. So that's what she did. She left me."

The tears started gushing before she could think of stopping them, so she covered her face with her hands. Her shoulders shook with the waves of grief she'd tried to hold back for too long.

Before Jessica could barely register the sharp creak of her aunt's chair, Lois was standing over her again. She hesitated for a second then lowered herself to the floor beside Jessica. She put an arm around Jessica's shoulder and pulled her close. "It's okay," Lois murmured. "It's going to be okay."

Jessica savored the warmth of the unexpected embrace for a

long moment before saying, "You were the one who wanted what was best for me, Aunt Lois. You stayed, and I could count on you. Everyone can because you're dependable. I don't want to run out on the people who need me. I want to be dependable too."

Lois replied with a soft chuckle. "Look, I know you're upset, but I'm fairly certain the answer isn't to make *me* your role model, hon."

Jessica smiled at the endearment then gave a watery laugh. "Maybe it is. Maybe I want to wear heels and sit in meetings and work in Town Hall."

"And referee feuding city council members?"

"That too."

They were both laughing in earnest now, and Lois gave Jessica's shoulder one last squeeze before releasing her.

Once they quieted down, Lois said, "You probably won't believe I'm saying this, but music, art—all those things are not just an impractical waste of time. You heard that video of Samuel. He was so talented. Sometimes when he sang, I felt like the whole world had righted itself. And he even tried to inspire my creative side too."

Jessica tried not to gawk. Lois had a creative side? "He did? What did you create?"

Lois looked away, and a pensive frown pinched her brow. "That was so long ago, Jessica. Maybe I'll tell you another time."

"Okay, sure," Jessica agreed, eager to preserve the newfound harmony between them. But it was impossible not to notice that, when she'd asked about her art, Lois had been completely closed off for the first time in weeks.

DREAMS LAST

25

For the second time in a month, Lois found herself in her car on the way to the roadhouse after an intense discussion with Jessica. But this time, there would be no turning around. This time, she truly didn't know what else to do.

When Jessica had gone to bed early—clearly worn out from their emotional conversation—Lois sat alone in the quiet living room reflecting on all they'd discussed. Watching Jessica fight through her grief over losing Rachel had been painful, but not nearly as painful as the girl's sudden attitude toward her music.

She was giving up. Walking away from something that, no matter what she thought or felt about it now, was a part of her very soul. It made Lois's stomach turn to mush, even more so, because she was partly responsible.

Not because of the accident. No, after some artful badgering from Jessica, Lois had promised not to blame herself for the accident anymore. But all those years of Lois never giving a single hint of encouragement to Jessica's music still remained. And now her niece held her up as some kind of paragon of practicality. The whole situation was deeply unsettling and the complete opposite of how it felt the world was supposed to be.

So, to the roadhouse she went, right after closing, like she had that night over a year ago. But now her frame of mind was entirely different. Now, she wasn't angry. She was desperate.

The main entrance of the building was still unlocked, so Lois stepped inside, but she called out to avoid startling anyone. Of course, her very presence there was startling, judging by the way Marty exited the kitchen then skidded to a stop as soon as she spotted Lois.

Lois forced what she hoped would pass for a natural smile. "Hi."

"Evening," Marty said, resuming her work. "How's Jess?"

"Well, that's why I'm here."

Marty set a tray of glasses down with a rattling thud and faced Lois, eyes wide with alarm.

"No, no, no," Lois reassured hastily. "She's fine. I didn't mean to imply she wasn't, it's just . . . well, can we talk for a minute?"

Marty's face relaxed to her neutral expression. "Sure." She pointed to a table. "You want something to drink? We make a mean glass of lemonade. Fresh squeezed. Or how about a grape soda? That's Jess's favorite."

"Okay, yeah. Thanks."

Marty set a glass bottle on the table, and they sat down. "Where's Barb?"

"Right here," Barb announced as she entered from the back. "Hello, Lois. What's going on with Jess?"

Lois took a sip of the soda and grimaced at the burst of sweetness. No wonder Jessica always used to have a cavity or two at her regular dental checkups. With a sigh, she set the bottle down and rested her elbows on the table. "She says she doesn't care about playing the guitar anymore. In fact, she sounds like she doesn't care about music at all."

Marty winced and looked away, and Barb shook her head and murmured, "Poor thing. She's been through so much." Barb's eyes met Lois's. "You see that, don't you? She's bound to feel and say a lot of things because of the grief and heartache she's experienced, but it will pass eventually. Her heart needs time to heal just like her hand did."

"But that's the problem," Lois said, "Her hand does need to heal, and she has to work at it *now* to get it in shape to play. This may be her only chance for that to happen. I don't want her to have regrets later. I want her to follow her—oh, for heaven's sakes!" She covered her forehead and groaned at the uncomfortable irony of what she'd been about to say.

"What's the matter?" Marty demanded.

Lois guffawed. "I was going to say 'I want her to follow her dreams.' This is the first time I've ever said it. You know that? Yeah, I'll bet you do. Jessica probably told you I never supported her music, even when I saw how talented she'd become. Now it's too late." Weariness seeped all the way through to her soul. "No matter what I do, I always end up failing the people I care about. I failed Jessica because I didn't give her enough encouragement, and I failed Samuel because I gave him too much."

Barb rested her hand on Marty's arm.

"Encouraged Sammy too much? Is that what you think?" Marty asked.

"Of course. I didn't know what was best for him! Yet that didn't stop me from prodding him on when he talked about leaving. I should have stayed out of it." Lois stared down at the table. "I've never admitted it to you, Marty, but I should have just stayed out of it. And I know it doesn't mean much, but I'm sorry. I'm sorry for what it cost both of you."

"Lois Connell, you look at me this instant," Marty snapped.

Oh, boy. Marty was really going to give her a piece of her mind now. Lois slowly raised her head and made eye contact with Marty. But there wasn't a trace of anger in the older woman's face.

"Lois, of all the people involved in what happened to Sammy, you are the only one *not* to blame, as far as I'm concerned."

"What?"

"You didn't give him the idea to leave town. He wanted to go; you said it yourself. And why did he want to go? Because his father and I tried to force him to be what *we* wanted him to be. But you were his true friend, Lois. You were the only one who loved and accepted him exactly as he was."

Eyes burning, Lois pictured Samuel's face. Yes, she'd loved him. They'd been like family. Even now, when she let herself think about him, it was hard to believe he was gone.

"Sammy used to say you were one of the most understanding people he knew, understanding, creative, and up for anything," Marty finished with a fond chuckle.

Lois toyed with her bottle and groaned. "I can't say I've been any of those things for a long time, maybe since he died. I mean, look at me! My whole life has been about finding a nice, respectable position in this town. All I care about is appearance and propriety and—I don't know—a bunch of other stuff that doesn't amount to much. What a joke."

"Survival isn't a joke, dear," Barb remarked, her expression grim.

"What do you mean?"

"I mean you got knocked down! You lost your friend, Joshua left, your sister turned on you. It all knocked you down, and you became what you had to just to make it through," Barb explained.

"That's what survivors do," Marty picked up the discussion again. "You, me, Barb: we're survivors. Just think about what I did. When my life fell apart, I bought a partnership in this tacky wasteland, as you call it."

Lois choked out a surprised laugh. "Yeah, sorry about that."

Marty waved the apology away and fixed her steady gaze on Lois. "But, at some point, we all have to ask ourselves the same thing: is survival enough?"

Lois took another sip of her syrupy beverage. Part of her wanted to feign ignorance and ask Marty what she was talking about, but she didn't. The question pierced straight to her heart.

Barb scooted closer and gave a gentle smile. "Finding out the answer may be your best chance of helping my granddaughter too."

****

The streets were empty as Lois drove back home, and without the distraction of traffic, Marty's question rolled through her mind over and over again. *Is survival enough?*

The longer she thought about it, the more it reminded her of something Joshua had said: that he'd come to a point in life where he wasn't okay just getting by anymore.

She'd been "getting by" for ages now. She'd stopped having dreams of the future, and she'd relished very little about the present. Her whole life was about insulating herself from the shame, chaos, and grief of the past, so she'd constructed an impenetrable fort of practicality and respectability. And no one was allowed in but her, not even her niece.

She pulled into the driveway and parked, her gaze traveling to the window of Jessica's upstairs room. Well, for years, she hadn't let Jessica in, yet somehow, the girl had finally managed to rattle the walls of Lois's fort.

Jessica didn't merely survive. She lived life with her whole heart. With all she'd been through, she was an unbelievably open and loving young woman. Despite the difficulties between them, Jessica had come back here, given of her time and her self to help Lois.

It was the same way Joshua seemed to give of himself to his students. It was evident in the way he spoke about them. His life was about so much more than "getting by" now.

And in their unconventional way, Marty and Barb were living fully and fiercely too by caring for their own unique community.

This fuller, deeper life seemed to be all around her now, and suddenly, she wanted it too.

But how?

She got out of the car and shut her door, but instead of going inside, she leaned against the hood. Tilting her head back, she looked up at the stars, artistic in their luminosity. When she was a child, she would watch the stars on summer nights. Standing under so much vast, open light and space, she would believe that anything was possible. And now, she believed it once again.

She drew in a long, shaky breath and closed her eyes. "God, I guess it's pretty clear that I've tried to build my life apart from you. I thought I could make things right on my own. I thought I could move on from the past without asking for help. But all I managed to do was push love away. Please forgive me."

Tears began to roll down her face. "I can't—I don't want to go on like this any longer. I need your grace. And I want to live and love fully the way you intended. I want abundant life. Please show me how."

Her prayer finished, she returned to watching the sky.

Deep silence mingled with the humid night air to enfold her. It seemed to buoy her in a kind of weightless harmony with the stars. Slowly, a profound sense of peace passed through her along with something else. Something she'd caught glimpses of in the past— when Joshua would hold her in his arms, when Samuel would play a new song for her, when Jessica tossed out one of her sarcastic little observations and grinned at Lois's reaction. They were all signposts pointing to something larger, more permanent. Something that could only be described as *joy*.

DREAMS LAST

26

A few days after her long talk with Lois, Jessica wandered past the window in the entryway of the house in time to catch sight of her aunt pulling into the driveway and exiting her car. Jessica paused to watch Lois. As she gathered her purse and briefcase, Lois's motions were quick and energetic, uncharacteristically lively considering she'd just come home from a long workday.

As soon as Lois entered the house, she flashed a wide smile at Jessica. "There you are. Guess what? I stopped by the PT center on the way home, and they gave me this." She held up several sheets of paper secured with a staple. "It's a list of exercises you can do here at home to strengthen your hand on the days when you don't have therapy."

The only response Jessica could manage was a nervous grin. The physical therapist had given her the same set of exercises, but she hadn't paid it much mind.

"So," Lois continued, "I thought I could help you work on these, and raise the speed limit on your road to recovery!"

Jessica's eyebrows shot up at Lois's colorful show of enthusiasm. "Aunt Lois this—this is really great of you, but I thought we talked about this the other night."

Lois gestured for Jessica to follow her to the living room, where they sat on the sofa.

"Look, Jessica," Lois began, her tone gentle, "I understand everything you said the other night, and I respect how you feel. But the thing is, you may not always feel that way."

Lois placed a hand on Jessica's shoulder. "You have a gift, Jessica. And I can't tell you how much I regret never paying more attention or telling you that sooner, but it's true. One day, you may find you want to pursue music again. Or maybe you'll simply want to play the guitar for your own enjoyment. And I don't want to see you have regrets about not working for that when you had the chance. So, please, can we do a few of these exercises on your off days?"

Jessica had studied her aunt while she was speaking, her heart radiating warmth when Lois had spoken of her musical gift. Did Lois really mean what she was saying? Or was this all about Lois still feeling responsible for the accident? In a few weeks, would things between them go back the way they'd always been?

"Can we negotiate?" Jessica asked abruptly.

Lois bit her lip. "Negotiate?"

"Yeah. How about I agree to work on this for the sake of my art," Jessica gestured at the sheet of exercises, "if you agree to tell me about *your* art."

Lois slid back a little, either in surprise or aversion to the suggestion; it was hard to say which. She fell silent for so long, Jessica began to suspect she was angry or upset. Then suddenly, Lois sat up straight and gave a firm nod. "Okay, you've got a deal."

They relocated to the kitchen table, and Jessica removed her hand brace to begin the first set of stretches and finger flexes. The pain was significantly less than it had been at the onset of her first PT session a few weeks before.

Lois watched for a few minutes, giving occasional pointers and encouragement, much like they'd both seen the therapists do. But for the most part, she was quiet until, a quarter of the way through the exercises, she murmured, "When I was in high school, I took an interest in photography. I collected all kinds of cameras, new and antique. I'd fix up the older ones and experiment with them sometimes, but I used the newer ones for most of my photos."

Intrigued, Jessica leaned forward, while momentarily forgetting to squeeze the rubber ball she was holding. "What kind of photos did you take?"

With a grin, Lois tapped the sheet of paper from the therapist until Jessica resumed her exercise. "My subjects were whatever I was in the mood to capture: people, old buildings, flowers, empty fields." Her face sobered. "I mostly stopped after that summer

Samuel died, except I'd take a few shots of town landmarks now and then."

"The pictures on your office wall!" Jessica blurted out. "Did you take those?"

Lois looked shocked. "Yes, those were mine."

"Wow, I had no idea." Jessica murmured. "I've always thought they were really cool, especially the one of that old cabin outside of town. Something about the way you captured the trees and overcast sky made it look haunted. Not in a scary way, though, but more like it was empty and crowded at the same time. Like it had a lot of history in its walls, and it was waiting for someone to come inside and find it."

"I had no idea you paid that much attention to those pictures," Lois said with a shake of her head.

Over the next week or so, Jessica found herself looking forward to each at-home exercise session because it meant Lois would keep sharing about her photography. She talked of long weekend drives—sometimes alone and sometimes with Joshua, Samuel, and Rachel—where she'd photograph whatever sites they'd find along the way.

She showed Jessica albums of her photos, including the one Jessica had found with the videotape. As it turned out, Lois had taken several shots of her sister, Samuel, and Joshua to fill the album. Each one unlocked a different memory, opening the door to a fuller, clearer understanding of their collective past. Lois had always been so guarded about events that had happened before Jessica was born, but not anymore.

Lois's willingness to share encouraged Jessica to do the same and, before long, she was telling her aunt all the things she hadn't bothered to discuss with her, especially things about the past year. Jessica described the strange, poignant road trip when she'd met Clifton and Darla. She talked about moving to New York and her life there, her work and her roommates.

Many of the stories that passed between them were painful, but surprisingly, almost as many were not. And every now and then, when she and Lois would laugh over some anecdote from Lois's teenage years or one of Jessica's odd encounters in New York City, Jessica would marvel at the beautiful absurdity of it all. She and Lois had lived in the same house for twelve years, but they hadn't actually known each other until now.

27

Lois huddled over her work computer and pounded at the keyboard until the ache in her shoulders forced her to stretch with a groan. Writing grant proposals was one of her least favorite aspects of her city manager role, but it was also a critical one. With the town's limited budget, grants were useful for filling funding gaps in important projects.

Lois rubbed her eyes, checked her watch, and gasped. 3:45? How could she have let the time get away from her like this? Jessica's PT appointment was in thirty minutes. She'd never make it home fast enough to get Jessica to the therapist's office in time.

Jessica could probably drive herself, but with her hand still in a brace, Lois would rather she didn't. Lois pursed her lips and tapped her fingers on her desk.

An immediate solution sprang to mind but she hesitated. Yes, Joshua had offered help for one thing or another numerous times over the last few weeks. He'd even stopped by her house a couple of times, suggesting some bit of yard work or home repair he could do for her. She'd declined his offers so far, but now . . .

Before she could second-guess the decision, Lois snatched up her cellphone and scrolled through her contacts to the number Joshua had recently given her.

Joshua answered on the second ring. "Lois, hi."

"Hi. Are you busy this afternoon? It's totally fine if you are. But I'm tied up here at the office and I can't make it back home in time to take Jessica to her physical therapy appointment at 4:15. I was wondering, if you happened to be close by and available, if maybe you wouldn't mind driving her?"

"Of course I can."

Lois didn't register his words at first, so she hurried on. "I normally wouldn't ask, obviously, I'd say she could reschedule or skip the appointment, but Jessica has been working so hard and making so much progress with her therapy that I hate to interrupt that momentum."

"I can understand that. Like I said, I'll give her a lift," he answered cheerfully.

"O-oh. You will?"

"Absolutely."

"You don't need to check your schedule or anything?"

"I did while you were explaining it to me."

Lois laughed. "Right. Okay, then. Thank you *so* much."

"It's not a problem. I'm happy to do it, Lois, really. If you can just let Jessica know to expect me, I'll head over there now."

Once Lois had ended the call and texted Jessica to apologize and inform her about the change of plans, she scooted back to her desk to resume her work. But her concentration was missing now.

Her thoughts kept returning to Joshua.

Truth be told, she'd longed to call him before this, but not to ask for a favor. She wanted to tell him she was beginning to understand what he meant about grace now. She wanted to talk to him about how things had been changing in her life. So many things.

She turned from her computer with a sigh and looked out the window.

Maybe she could ask Joshua for another favor, something that would require them to spend time together. Here in the quiet solitude of her office, she could admit how much she wished she and Joshua were close enough to talk again.

But after that first, intense discussion at the hospital, Joshua had given no indication of pursuing that kind of friendship with her. His sole concern seemed to be "making things right." What had he said? He wouldn't be able to move forward if he didn't.

Move forward. What did that mean? Going back to Chicago, most likely. Was he in a relationship back there? Was he ready to make a commitment to another woman but felt he needed to finally close the Lois chapter of his life first? The thought made her heart sink like a leaky boat in a pond.

But she had no right to those feelings. Nor did she have the right to keep Joshua from his future, whatever it might hold. No, the most loving thing she could do now was encourage Joshua to embrace his freedom to move forward.

****

Lois leaned back in her desk chair and blew out an exhausted breath. "Finally," she muttered.

"Rough day?"

Her heart skipped unexpectedly when she looked up to see Joshua leaning against her office doorframe and grinning at her.

"Joshua, hey. What are you doing here? Do I need to get Jessica?"

He laughed. "Her physical therapy was over an hour ago, Lois."

"Oh, my gosh. I can't believe I let the time fly by again." She rubbed her head then scrambled to shove folders in her briefcase. "Great. And I told Jessica I'd make an early dinner tonight. She's gotta be so annoyed by now."

Joshua walked further in and held up a hand. "Hey, hey. Relax, okay? I can assure you Jessica isn't annoyed in the least. She told me all about how you were working on a big project today and would probably be too—to use her words—'in the zone' to remember your own name. So, she asked me to take her over to see Marty and Barb, and she'd grab dinner there."

Lois relaxed back into her chair and chuckled. "I think she's onto me."

"So it would seem." He held up a paper bag she hadn't noticed him carrying and shook it. "You should probably eat too, you know. I got some to-go food when I dropped Jessica off. Baker made catfish tonight."

The briny, deep fried aroma wafted toward her, making her stomach rumble. Had she remembered to eat lunch today?

"That's really nice of you, Joshua, but you didn't have to."

He shrugged one shoulder. "I know, but I wanted to. Listen, I got myself some food too. Is there a place around here we could eat?"

She nodded and, a few minutes later, they were sitting at a small conference table that was now serving as a dining table.

Conversation flowed easily between them as they talked about

Jessica, their respective jobs, and even a few of the major news events that had occurred over the years they'd been apart. It was an odd mixture of familiarity and newness.

But as they finished their meal, the pressure of her earlier reflections about Joshua's future began to build, pushing on her head from the inside until her temples ached.

Joshua must have noticed a shift in her behavior because he asked, "Lois, is anything wrong?"

She closed her eyes for a second, both to dull the effect his piercing blue eyes had on her heart and to send up a quick prayer for strength. This was the best thing, the right thing.

Opening her eyes again, she contrived a smile. "Nothing is wrong, but there's something I need to say to you, Joshua."

He wiped his hands on his jeans. "Okay."

"I appreciate how hard it must have been for you to come back here after all these years. I appreciate how hard you've worked to make peace between us and to show me you regret leaving." She drew a deep breath, hoping he didn't notice how it trembled. "But you don't need to do anything else, as far as I'm concerned. I forgive you, Joshua. I do. And I don't want you to feel obliged to stick around here as some kind of penance. You have a life back in Chicago."

A real smile replaced her earlier forced one. "All those bright kids of yours still need you."

"There are bright kids here too."

Everything inside her went still. "What?"

He leaned a bit closer, elbows resting on his knees. "I'm gonna have to level with you, Lois. I really thought coming back here was about trying to make things right with you. And it was. But then I saw you again." He took off his glasses, fixing his sapphire blue eyes on her and drawing her in.

"I can't stand the thought of leaving you again. Lois, I still love you. I don't think I stopped for a second in all these years. And I know it could take a long time to earn back your trust enough for you to love me again. Maybe I never can. But I'm asking if you could give me a chance to try."

Lois could only sit, frozen in place for a moment. It was all so much: his confession, his request, and his vulnerable, searching expression. How in the world had they gotten here after nearly twenty years?

Some tiny, stubbornly pragmatic corner of her brain declared things could never work between them after so much time. But her heart refused to listen. She still loved Joshua too. There was no point in denying it. Now all she needed to do was tell him she'd agree to give him his chance. A nice, measured response, true enough to her heart to get by, without risking too much.

But, no, that sounded like the old Lois. Gratitude and joy thrummed on her heartstrings. The new Lois didn't *do* half measures.

Without a word, Lois sprang from her chair and leaned down to press a fervent kiss to Joshua's lips.

He tensed, as if in shock, for a whole three seconds. Then his arms slid around to pull her close.

When they finally pulled apart, his smile shone but his eyes were suspiciously damp. "It's so good to finally be home."

28

Jessica polished off her last piece of cornbread and scooted back from the table with a sigh of contentment. Baker appeared by her table to pick up her plate. He smirked down at her. "Jess, you didn't come here for a catfish dinner. You came here for coleslaw and cornbread."

She laughed. "I can't help it, Baker. You make the best. You think I can get slaw like this in New York?"

Baker shuddered. "Girl, it's a miracle you don't starve to death up there."

As Baker shuffled off, Jessica looked around and leaned into the quiet. She'd always loved coming in for a bite to eat in the late afternoon before the dinner and late night crowd showed up. It was a good time and place to think or talk things over with Marty and Barb.

As if sensing her reflections, Barb came in from the back. When Jessica turned to speak to her, she noticed a guitar case leaning against the wall. Jessica pointed to the instrument. "Hey, do you guys have someone playing here regularly now?"

"Oh, no, that's mine," Barb replied offhandedly before pouring herself a glass of lemonade.

"Yours?" Jessica stood up and faced Barb. "You never told me you played!"

"Lemonade?" Barb handed her a glass.

Jessica accepted the glass and set it down with a thud. "Barb!"

"What?"

"You've never said a word about playing the guitar."

Barb shrugged, but her nonchalance didn't cover the tiny grin that played on the corner of her lips as she said, "Well, sure. Where do you think you inherited your musical talent?"

Jessica started to sputter, but before she could come up with any kind of response, Marty entered the room looking amused, as if she'd overheard the exchange between Jessica and Barb. "Oh, yeah. Barb here used to perform at the local festivals and fairs back in the day." Marty smiled at Barb. Her tone grew distant, as if lost in a memory. "We didn't really know each other then, but I do remember how she could pull in a crowd."

"When did you stop performing?" Jessica asked.

"I guess it was around the time I got married and had Don. Don's father ran off when he was four and left me with this place. I didn't have much time for music after that. Since then, I've only really played for myself from time to time."

Jessica swallowed. The last thing she wanted was to make Barb uncomfortable, but she was dying to ask. "Well, w-would you play for me?"

Barb cast a glance at Marty, who lowered her brows and gave a firm, encouraging nod. *Strange.* Had Marty put Barb up to this?

"Please, Barb?" Jessica pleaded.

Barb reached up and pressed a warm hand to Jessica's cheek. "Okay, for you."

Taking the guitar from its case, Barb sat down to tune it for a few minutes. Then she started playing, softly at first then louder, as if she were getting a feel for the instrument again.

The first few chords were exploring and improvisational before transitioning into the intro of a song. Jessica only had to listen for a second to recognize the tune of the Grateful Dead's "Ripple." There had been several former "Deadheads" among the roadhouse customers when Jessica used to play here, and this was one of their favorites.

Barb began to sing, and Jessica moved closer to sit, her heart soaring with Barb's gentle, melodic voice. Barb tilted her head at Jessica in a welcoming gesture, so Jessica began to sing the harmony. Their gazes held as their voices naturally blended together. Sudden gratitude swept through Jessica's spirit for the simple, unexpected joy of singing with her grandmother.

When the song ended, several sets of hands began to clap.

Jessica looked up in surprise to see Baker, Curly, and a couple of customers applauding. But Marty, tough talking, no-nonsense Marty, was simply watching, eyes glistening and one hand pressed over her heart.

A few minutes later, Jessica and Barb stepped outside away from the growing clamor of customers.

"How many years has it been since you played for an audience?" Jessica asked.

"Nearly forty years."

"Too long," Jessica murmured with a shake of her head.

Barb planted her hands on her hips. "No, I'd say it's been too long since *you've* played for an audience, Jess."

Jessica sucked in a breath of the humid evening air. "I think it's gonna rain soon. Maybe we should go inside."

"Jess, listen to me." Barb's tone turned firm. "Do you remember when you first started visiting us? When you started playing out here for the customers?"

Jessica nodded.

"You weren't just messing around. You did this for years. Why? What was it that made you keep coming back? Why'd you work so hard and practice and learn all the different songs these old fogies requested? Why'd you do it?"

Closing her eyes, Jessica pictured standing out there on the deck, playing in front of a couple dozen customers that first time. The odd assortment of people had unnerved her at first, but as she played and sang, she'd begun studying their faces. Some looked tired, some depressed, some merely looked bored with life. But as she continued to perform, they started smiling. They would even laugh when, in between songs, she'd make some silly joke or self-deprecating quip. When the crowd had applauded, she'd been gratified, but the real thrill had come from watching the collective mood of the group lift for a while.

"I realized the music I made could have the same effect on other people as it did on me. When I found it soothing or comforting, they did too. When I was happy, so were they. Whenever I was out here playing—I don't know—we all just connected."

Jessica took a seat at the nearest picnic table bench. How had she forgotten that?

Barb sat down beside her and put an arm around her shoulders.

"The ability to touch people's hearts with your music is a God-given gift. I saw it that very first day you played for us. That's what matters. Never mind if it's 'in your blood' or not. Never mind what I or your mom or your aunt or anybody else wants you to do. God gave the gift to you, Jess Connell. And it's up to you to decide if you'll share it."

Barb gave Jessica a quick hug and stood up. "I'd better get back in there before we get so busy that Marty decides to take over everything and make Curly and Baker cry again." She took a conspiratorial tone and winked. "That's *her* gift."

Jessica laughed as Barb went inside.

The wind started to pick up, blowing bits of dust and stray blades of grass around her. Then a fine curtain of mist began to fall. Jessica rose from her place on the bench to go inside but stopped when the soft, delicate droplets hit her face. Closing her eyes, she savored the sweet, cleansing feel of it.

A gift.

Despite the grief of the last year, there had been many gifts. She'd met Clifton and Darla, started a life in New York, and now . . . now she'd discovered the truth about her past, and was beginning to have the kind of relationship with her aunt she'd always wanted.

Jessica opened her eyes and looked down at her injured hand with a snicker. The last two gifts had more or less been the result of her accident. Whoever said God worked in mysterious ways must have lived through a few weeks like she'd just had. And it seemed God was offering her yet another gift: the chance for her hand to heal enough for her to play the guitar again.

Closing her eyes once more, she tilted her head up toward the misty sky. "Lord, thank you. Thank you for all of these gifts, even the ones I didn't recognize at first. Thank you for the people you've put in my life; thank you for putting me in theirs. And thank you—" Jessica released a sob. "Thank you for allowing me to make music. Whether or not I make a full recovery or not, I want to place it in your hands. Please help me use all the abilities you've given me to show your love."

She spent a few minutes breathing in the rain soaked air and the sense of serenity that settled deep in her spirit.

29

Jessica's heart was thudding with the rhythmic force of an epic drum solo as she paced the tiny office in the back of the roadhouse where she'd gone to prepare.

"Come on, Jess, chill," she muttered under her breath. "It's just another day at the roadhouse." But it was a Saturday in summer at the roadhouse. At lunchtime, there could be up to thirty customers at one time, milling around at the outdoor tables. It would be the biggest group of people she'd played for since her accident.

For the past few weeks, she'd doubled down on her physical therapy and practiced her guitar playing with Barb. She'd even played for the dinner crowd several times. But that had mostly been a matter of giving a little ambience, some background noise for the diners. If things were like they used to be, the Saturday group would be more attentive, making the whole thing feel closer to an actual performance.

She gave her head a sharp shake and sat down to tune her guitar. There was no point in psyching herself out. Even if it was a performance, it was only a little one. Not like a concert with a bunch of different—

A firm rap on the office door interrupted her reflections. It was probably Marty or Barb. "Come in," she called before returning her attention to her tuning pegs.

"It sure is quiet around here. I thought there was gonna be some live music," a voice drawled from the doorway.

Jessica's head bobbed up. "Clifton!" She sprang to her feet and hurried to hug him. "What are you doing here?"

"I was getting tired of emails, so I decided to come down in person and see if you're really working," he teased.

Jessica chuckled before letting out a very unmusical squeal as she spotted Darla right behind Clifton.

Darla walked in the room and placed her hands on Jessica's shoulders with a frown. "Let me have a look at you."

"You've seen me on video calls every week!"

Darla waved the comment away and studied Jessica's face, her piercing gaze searching Jessica inside and out. Finally, Darla grinned. "You look like you're in one piece to me." She pulled Jessica into a tight hug and murmured, "It's an answer to our prayers."

Jessica returned the embrace then gaped over Darla's shoulder as two more figures approached the office. It was Natalie and Glenn.

"I can't believe it!" Jessica said as more hugs were exchanged.

Natalie beamed. "This is your comeback, Jessica. We wouldn't miss that."

"Yeah, besides," Glenn chimed in with his heavy Jersey accent. "It's a nice vacation. I've never been to Texas."

"Never?" Jessica asked.

"Nope. If the subway or PATH doesn't run there, neither do I. Know what I'm sayin'?"

They all laughed until Darla spoke up. "Okay, everyone, let's go outside and let Jessica finish getting ready."

The group of friends clamored out with admirable haste, leaving Jessica alone. Still stunned, she shuffled out of the office and made her way to the side door closest to the outdoor space where she'd be playing.

All at once, she became aware of how much noise was circulating outside the building. She peeked out the closest window and was shocked at the number of cars in the parking lot. There were at least twice as many as she'd ever seen here in the past.

Several people were approaching the building together. She squinted to see them better and gasped. It was Reverends Murphy and June along with their respective spouses. As they walked, they chatted with a silver-haired man who looked suspiciously like— "Mayor Dawson!" She said it aloud.

Lois appeared at her side then and Jessica turned to her. "Aunt

Lois, why is the mayor here? And people from the church too! What's going on?"

"I invited them," Lois answered serenely.

"Y-you invited them to the roadhouse?"

"Absolutely." Lois faced her, tenderness in her tone and expression. "I told all my friends that my talented niece was performing today, and I wanted them to come watch."

Tears sprang to Jessica's eyes. No, no. She couldn't bawl before a gig. With effort, she blinked back the flood and threw her arms around Lois.

Lois held her close. "I am so, so proud of you."

"I haven't done anything yet," Jessica warbled.

"It doesn't matter. I'm proud of you now. Just the way you are."

30

Lois stepped into the blazing sunlight outside the roadhouse and made her way to the bench where Joshua had saved her a seat right beside him. But she nearly jumped back up at the boisterous applause—particularly from the regular patrons—that greeted Jessica as she stepped onto the small platform in front of the tables.

Jessica adjusted the microphone that had been set up on the platform, her face unnaturally still. Lois's pulse thumped a nervous beat, and she matched it with the tapping of her fingers on her lap. Was Jessica really up to this? Was it too soon? Had Lois made a mistake inviting all the extra people? Maybe it would have been better to—

Joshua reached over and took her hand in his, serving to silence her runaway thoughts. Their eyes met, and he offered her a knowing smile that comforted and thrilled in equal parts. Calmer now, she returned her focus to her niece.

As if some internal switch had flipped, Jessica's face lit up in a smile. She made a show of scanning the crowd and quipped, "Woo! Look at all these faces. I always said once word got out about how tasty Curly and Baker's Saturday barbeque is, there'd be a big crowd here!"

Everyone laughed.

Jessica's eyes softened. "Seriously, though, it's amazing to see everyone here today. You're all very special, and you've been a huge help to Aunt Lois this past month or so with the flood and my accident. I'm deeply grateful for all that you've done and all that you are, so I'm glad to have this chance, in my small way, to thank you."

The speech was met with applause that Lois almost forgot to join in on until the last minute. She was too impressed by how natural and gracious Jessica was in front of the group.

"Okay, let's get started," Jessica said. "You folks sit back and enjoy the barbeque—which really is scrumptious, by the way—and someone tell me what I'm singing first."

Lois frowned. That was an odd way to start. But the crowd was only quiet for a moment before a seventy-something man seated off to the side shouted, "Can't Help Falling!"

"Whoa!" Jessica playfully staggered back a step. "'The King' for my very first song? You sure about that, Dean?"

Dean grinned and started clapping, along with several others at his table.

"Whatever you say," she smiled at the man then addressed the rest of the group. "As I'm sure you all know, 'Can't Help Falling in Love,' popularized by the great Elvis Presley, is an oldie, so feel free to sing along, if you want."

She started out a little softly, eyes focused on her guitar strings, and Lois once again fretted that this all might be happening too soon. But, a second later, Jessica raised her head and her voice grew stronger, her expression sweet as she sang. People all around Lois were swaying in time with the song, and many began to sing along, with Jessica's encouragement.

"I'd say the crowd can't help falling in love with Jessica."

Lois glanced to her left to see that Jessica's friend Natalie had sat down in a folding chair beside her.

"I think you're right," Lois acknowledged.

Natalie shook her head. "She's really got *it*, you know? If that guy from the Solstice Riddles could've seen her with an audience, he would have snapped her up in a second."

Lois nodded. Jessica had told her about the audition. She'd tried to downplay it, but it wasn't hard to see how much it had crushed her.

"Their former singer came back, right?" Lois asked.

"Pfft. The rumor is she's a bit of a diva. She's already split again. That spot is wide open now." Natalie raised an eyebrow at Lois and went back to watching Jessica.

Lois's mind began to spin. Did Jessica still have a shot with this band? Even if she didn't, would she be ready to keep trying? In either case, it would mean she'd be going back to New York.

Lois bit her lip. Jessica would leave. It was the best thing for her; she had prospects and friends and community there. Lois wouldn't begrudge her that. But at the same time, a tiny worry began to nag her. Would things between her and Jessica go back the way they were before her visit? No calls, no checking in, and very little news? It seemed like an unreasonable scenario, given everything that had happened over the last month and a half, but still Lois worried.

Applause rang out for Jessica's first song, even as multiple requests trickled in for the second song. Some voices called out specific titles; others just shouted band or singer names. Jessica knew them all. One minute, she was singing a snappy tune from a contemporary country band Lois wasn't familiar with, and the next, she was playing a slow, soothing rendition of the Beatles classic "All You Need is Love."

"Your niece is a human jukebox," Joshua said, leaning close.

"Mm-hmm."

He took her hand again. "Hey, is everything okay?"

Everything was changing, actually. Whether that was okay or not still remained to be seen. It was all so much. Sitting here, holding hands with the man she'd never dreamed of seeing or touching again, neither of them the same people they were all those years ago, but still connected on a level that defied all common sense. Watching Jessica: the shy, often melancholy little girl she'd raised standing up there, a grown woman, smiling, playing, and working the crowd like she was born to do it. Where was it all going? The question filled her with nervous anticipation.

"Lois, look at me," Joshua murmured.

When she did, he searched her eyes the way he used to when they were younger, as if he were trying to read her thoughts. More often than not, he was successful.

"Have faith, okay?" he said. "Things are going fast, but they're working out. God is working them out. And whatever happens, from now on, I'll be by your side for as long as you want me."

Tingling warmth pulsed all the way through Lois, starting where their two hands were joined. She lifted Joshua's hand and brushed her lips across his knuckles. "I'm gonna hold you to that."

He leaned in for a quick kiss just before the crowd erupted in more applause.

"Thank you!" Jessica said. "How about one more fast one? Any suggestions?"

A small voice near the back shouted, "Put Your Records On!"

Lois searched the faces until she spotted Baker with a little girl sitting on his shoulders. She appeared to be six or seven and sported an adorable profusion of braids.

Jessica beamed. "Is that Corinne Baker I see over there? Baker, bring her over here, please."

As soon as Baker got close, the little girl reached out for Jessica. Swinging her guitar behind her, Jessica took the child and grinned. "You've gotten so big this year!" She faced the crowd. "Folks, this is Baker's granddaughter, Corinne. Her mama named her after the singer Corinne Bailey Rae. And what's her best song, C?"

"Put Your Records On!" Corinne yelled gleefully.

"That's right! Let's do it." She set the girl down and started playing the breezy, cheerful tune. During the chorus, little Corinne danced along, clapping in time with the music. Jessica swayed in step with the girl as she sang, her voice exuberant and free. By the final chorus, the whole crowd was clapping along.

When the song was over, there were whistles and shouts coming from every direction.

"Natalie, did you get that one?"

Lois was startled to see Darla make her way through the tables and approach Natalie, who was holding her phone up in the air.

"I got the whole last song!" Natalie said triumphantly.

"Great!" Darla replied. "Now that dodo bird with the Solstice Riddles can see Jessica in her element. This is what she was meant to do."

Lois turned and watched Jessica thanking people and shaking hands, so vibrant and joyful. Yes, this was what Jessica was meant to do. This was her living the abundant life she was called to live, and no matter what, Lois wouldn't stand in the way of it again.

****

Two Weeks Later

Lois helped Joshua unload the final boxes of his belongings from the moving van and into the storage unit he'd temporarily rented after moving from Chicago. While he locked up the unit, Lois looked over the fence at the roadhouse and caught sight of Marty standing outside, so she waved.

She paused to take in the striking beauty of the day. Plush cumulus clouds spotted the sky. Against the brilliant blue backdrop, the old roadhouse didn't seem decrepit, for once. It had character: resilience and hardiness. Lois went to the truck and pulled out the camera she'd taken to keeping near her again. She took shots of the roadhouse from a few different angles.

When she was finished, Joshua approached and put an arm around her shoulders. "Wanna go over there for some dinner? Thanks to Jessica, you, Marty, and Barb always seem to have plenty to talk about these days."

"Why not? I'd love to hear their thoughts on the latest developments."

"So the band really took Jessica on without even asking for another audition?" Joshua asked.

"That's right. Natalie sent that video of Jessica playing here to her contact for the Solstice Riddles, they watched it, and reached out to Jessica right away. That's why she had to fly back to New York this morning."

"You think she's ready?"

"I know she is," Lois affirmed with a nod. Still, her stomach sank a little. Jessica was going to have to get to work with the band almost as soon as she arrived. Who knew how long it would be before she heard from her next?

Holding hands, Lois and Joshua made their way next door, but before they got far, Lois's cellphone rang. She stopped and glanced at the screen.

It was Jessica.

Breathing a prayer of thanks, she answered, but before she could get out a greeting, Jessica said, "Hi, Aunt Lois, have you set a date yet?"

Lois frowned. "Hi to you too, and a date for what?"

"For when you and Joshua are getting married, of course!"

"Jessica!" Lois laughingly scolded, her face heating.

"What? We both know it's going to happen. Why so embarrassed? Oh . . . is he there with you now? Put him on, and I'll ask him myself."

"Je-ss-i-ca, stop!" The incorrigible girl was clearly enjoying this a little too much.

"Okay, okay. I'll stop. I'm just calling to let you know that I made it back to the City safe and sound."

Lois's heart soared. "I appreciate that."

"I'll call you again soon when I get some more details, but I've already gotten a peek at the touring schedule and, guess what? We'll be playing in Texas in a couple of months."

"That's great, Jessica! That means we'll get to see you, right?"

"Right. And since I'll be there anyway," she assumed a sing-song voice, "it would be a great time to schedule a wedding."

"Jessica, I'm warning you!" Lois tried and failed to make her voice sound imposing. What was the point? Joshua had hinted about marriage several times already, but they hadn't settled it yet. If she thought about it, two months didn't seem like an impossibility.

Jessica's buoyant giggles floated through the phone. "All right, I guess I'll leave y'all to figure that out. Besides, I've got enough to think about with this tour."

"Are you nervous?"

"Nervous? No. Excited? Yes. Slightly panic-stricken? Definitely," she admitted wryly.

Lois laughed. "Those sound like perfectly natural feelings. I'm sure it will be scary at first. But it's also going to be amazing, and so are you."

There was silence on the other end for a moment. When Jessica spoke again, her tone was low. "Thank you, Aunt Lois. I wouldn't be here now if it weren't for you. I really owe you."

"No! You don't owe me anything. Just promise you'll be careful out there and use your head, and that'll be good enough for me."

"I promise," Jessica said with a warm chuckle. "Now, I should probably go. I'll call again soon, and I'll email the tour schedule once it's finalized too."

"That would be great."

"Okay, bye."

"Bye." Lois started to lower the phone then raised it again at the last second. "Jessica?"

"Yes?"

"I love you."

There was another beat of silence then a soft sniffle. "I love you too, Aunt Lois."

155

The End

THANK YOU!

Dear reader

I hope you enjoyed Jessica and Lois's story, and that it encouraged you in your own personal walk with the Lord. You'll find further inspiration and encouragement on The Potter's House Books Website, (www.pottershousebooks.com) and by reading the other books in the series. Read them all and be encouraged and uplifted!

Find all the books on Amazon and on The Potter's House Books website.

If you enjoyed *Dreams Last* please consider leaving a review on Amazon or Goodreads.

I'd also love to connect on Facebook, Twitter, or BookBub. Also, don't forget to check out my author newsletter, where I talk about my books and the books and authors I admire.

Blessings!

Chloe

ACKNOWLEDGMENTS

Wow! I can't believe the Potter's House Series 2 has come to a close. Sometimes when I'm spreading the word about the series and the latest book to release, I still can't believe I've been blessed to share space with these talented, spirit-filled authors. I am so grateful for each of them and for Becky, our amazing virtual assistant. I'm also grateful for Marion for the cover design and Ben Fenwick for the proofreading and endless well of support.

My family, brothers and sisters in Christ, and friends have been so, so supportive of my writing, and I can't express how much that has meant to me. In addition, I owe a giant THANKS! and a virtual hug to my early readers, including Valerie, Wendy, Paula, Kimberly, Trudy, and Erin. You all didn't just read the story; you helped me make it better. (Wendy, you've patiently read the first version of SIX of my books now: two whole series! You are a reading rock star!) I also want to thank my amazing early reviewer friends for all the enthusiasm and encouragement.

Most importantly, I thank God for leading me on this journey and opening my eyes to radical love and boundless grace every step of the way.

DREAMS LAST

ABOUT THE AUTHOR

Chloe S. Flanagan is an author, technical writer, blogger, and graduate of New York University. She enjoys exploring the Christian walk frankly and thoughtfully in her fiction and in her blog, The Candid Corinthian. When she's not writing, Chloe loves music, travel, reading books in all genres, and spending time with family.

Other books by Chloe S. Flanagan:

An Offer of Grace: A Christian Romantic Suspense Series

Forward to What Lies Ahead

A Time for Every Matter

No Longer a Stranger

www.ingramcontent.com/pod-product-compliance
Lightning Source LLC
Chambersburg PA
CBHW071422150726

48000CB00001B/443